YAWN…
Mmmmm… It's nice down here.
So dark and peaceful…
YAWN…
… And quiet…
You can just watch the fishes swim
by for hours until slowly, slowly,
v e r y slowly, your eyes start to feel…
YAWN…
… sleepy…
You close them for a moment – just for a
moment – and listen to the gentle blub,
blub, blub of the bubbles and…
YAWN…
… you find yourself drifting…
YAWN…
… off to sleep…
… And before you know it…
YAWN…
… you've been asleep down here for
years and years and years and
yearsssssszzzzzzzzzzzzzzzzzzz…

Mr Penguin's adventures began in:

ALEX T. SMITH

h HODDER

Mr Penguin is a penguin.

If you aren't sure whether he is one or not,
all you have to do is look at him.
Here he is now.

He *looks* like a penguin.

He is all black and white with a little beak
and two flappy flippers. When he walks, his
bottom wiggles about in *exactly* the sort of
way a penguin's bottom *should* wiggle.
But there's something rather unusual about
Mr Penguin. You see, he isn't
JUST a penguin.

He is an *Adventurer!*

He has the dashing hat, enormous magnifying glass and battered satchel – with a nice packed lunch of fish finger sandwiches inside – to prove it.

Mr Penguin's best friend is this spider. His name is Colin. He's really good at kung fu, so you'd better watch out! KAPOW!

That woman with the headscarf – she's called Edith Hedge. She's Mr Penguin's other best friend. The pigeon on her head is Gordon. He doesn't say much.

Together, they've been on two thrilling adventures already. Are you ready to join them on another?

This book is for Captain Arthur Everett,
and his mummy and daddy Danielle and Tom

HODDER CHILDREN'S BOOKS
First published in Great Britain in 2019 by Hodder and Stoughton

1 3 5 7 9 10 8 6 4 2

Text and illustrations copyright © Alex T. Smith, 2019

The moral rights of the author have been asserted.

A CIP catalogue record for this book is available from the British Library.

978-1-444-94458-7

Design by Alison Still

Printed and bound in China by Toppan Leefung Printing Limited.

The paper and board used in this book are made from wood from
responsible sources.

Hodder Children's Books
A division of Hachette Children's Group
Carmelite House, 50 Victoria Embankment, London EC4Y 0DZ

An Hachette UK Company
www.hachette.co.uk

CONTENTS

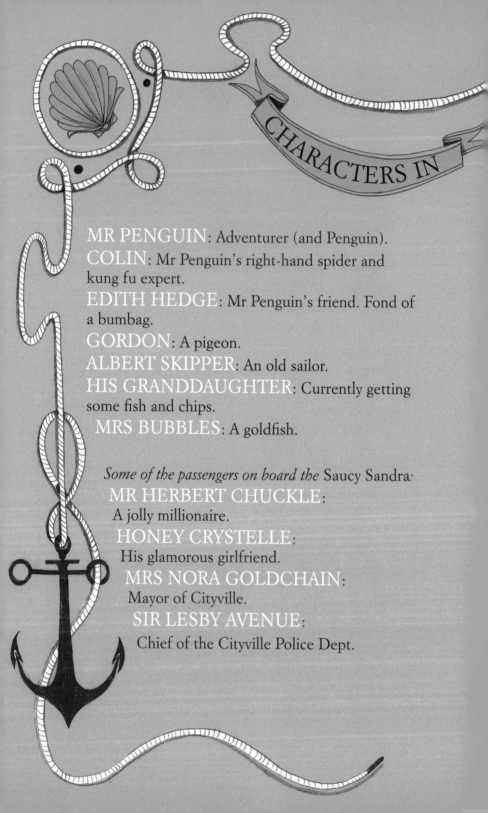

MR PENGUIN: Adventurer (and Penguin).

COLIN: Mr Penguin's right-hand spider and kung fu expert.

EDITH HEDGE: Mr Penguin's friend. Fond of a bumbag.

GORDON: A pigeon.

ALBERT SKIPPER: An old sailor.

HIS GRANDDAUGHTER: Currently getting some fish and chips.

MRS BUBBLES: A goldfish.

Some of the passengers on board the Saucy Sandra:

MR HERBERT CHUCKLE:
A jolly millionaire.

HONEY CRYSTELLE:
His glamorous girlfriend.

MRS NORA GOLDCHAIN:
Mayor of Cityville.

SIR LESBY AVENUE:
Chief of the Cityville Police Dept.

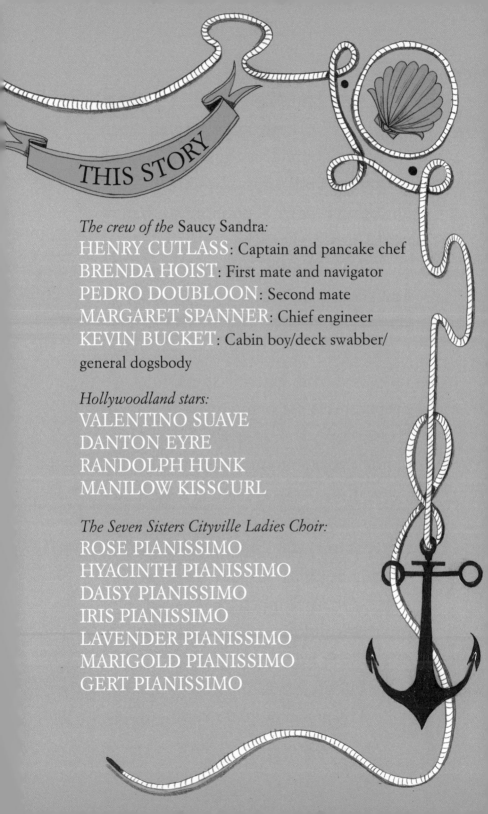

THIS STORY

The crew of the Saucy Sandra:
HENRY CUTLASS: Captain and pancake chef
BRENDA HOIST: First mate and navigator
PEDRO DOUBLOON: Second mate
MARGARET SPANNER: Chief engineer
KEVIN BUCKET: Cabin boy/deck swabber/
general dogsbody

Hollywoodland stars:
VALENTINO SUAVE
DANTON EYRE
RANDOLPH HUNK
MANILOW KISSCURL

The Seven Sisters Cityville Ladies Choir:
ROSE PIANISSIMO
HYACINTH PIANISSIMO
DAISY PIANISSIMO
IRIS PIANISSIMO
LAVENDER PIANISSIMO
MARIGOLD PIANISSIMO
GERT PIANISSIMO

W hat a night!

A storm is grumbling over Cityville. Thunder is thundering, wind is winding and rain is absolutely chucking it down – no more so than over Cityville Docks.

It is a Friday, exactly 7.18 p.m. and already dark. As always (and despite the weather) the docks are terrifically busy. Cargo is being loaded and unloaded from gigantic ships, final preparations are being made to a luxury cruise ship which is setting sail on its maiden voyage tomorrow.

In the doorway of his little house (a wooden fisherman's hut squished between two warehouses) a man is peering out into the rain. This man is called Albert Skipper. He has a nice hat, but that's not important right now. Albert isn't thinking about hats.

He's worried.

His granddaughter should have

been here exactly eighteen minutes ago but she hasn't arrived. Every Friday night she comes to his house with hot chips and they eat them from the newspaper they're wrapped in (saves washing up) and tell each other stories. Often Albert sings old sea shanties.

Hmmmmm, thinks Albert, she's probably just sheltering from the rain. Unless…

Oh dear. That "Unless dot dot dot" is actually rather worrisome…

Albert shakes the thought from his head and goes back inside. His granddaughter will be there in a minute. She'll be soaked through so he puts a blanket to warm in front of the stove for her. Then he spoons tea leaves into the pot and sets about feeding his goldfish. Her name is Mrs Bubbles.

But as he reaches for the tin of fish food, his eyes fall on the letter that arrived that morning. It was popped

silently under the door when he was
still asleep.

With the others that have been
delivered over the past few months, he's
just read them and then thrown them
into the stove, but this one is different.
It's more Worrying and Concerning. For
one thing it talks about Marina…

Suddenly, there is a knock at the door.
KNOCK KNOCK!

Aha! That will be his granddaughter
now! Thank goodness!

Decisively, he rips up the letter and
shoves most – but not all – of the little
pieces into the lining of his hat, puts it
on his head again and opens the door
with a big smile.

The smile doesn't last long.

It is not his granddaughter. It is a
great big shadowy person.

"I told you!" says Albert firmly. "I
won't do it!"

But before he can say any more, the

great big shadowy person picks Albert up (his nice hat and the tin of fish food fall to the floor) and plonks him into a great big wooden crate on wheels. Then the great big shadowy person shoves the crate and they both disappear into the night.

A few quiet minutes tick by…

Mrs Bubbles swims around in circles in her bowl. She's hungry.

Just then the door bursts open and in skids a soggy girl in slippy plimsolls.

It's Albert's granddaughter! (If only she'd arrived a few minutes sooner!)

"Sorry I'm late, Grampa!" she says, pulling a big parcel of chips in newspaper out from where she's been storing them (up her jumper). "I had to hide from the rai—"

She doesn't finish that sentence because suddenly she sees the mess – the fish food on the floor and her grampa's hat beside it. Her eyes are on stalks!

Leaping lobsters – what's happened?! she thinks.

Her grampa never goes ANYWHERE without his hat. He's had it since he was a sailor all those years ago...

It's then that she notices a tiny ripped bit of paper (it's from the torn-up letter, but she doesn't know that).

She picks it up. There's a word on it – well, part of a word. She's seen it before. Not long ago, in fact. It was written large on a board.

The girl scoops up some fish food and plops it into Mrs Bubbles' bowl, piles her box braids up on top of her head and hides them under her grampa's hat. She furrows her brow, does up her shoelaces and then she too disappears off into the night.

WHERE IS EVERYONE GOING?!

CHAPTER ONE

ALL ABOARD THE
SAUCY SANDRA!

There was a sudden loud and VERY hearty PAAAAAAAAAAARPPPP!

Edith Hedge stood with her pigeon on her head and her hands on her bumbag and took a great big sniff.

"Smell that, Mr Penguin?" she cried, her eyes watering slightly. "Isn't it wonderful!"

Now, before I get into trouble, the PARP wasn't THAT sort of PARP, you dirty scoundrels. Edith was actually taking a sniff of the fresh, blustery sea smell sweeping in briskly across the docks and shimmying up her nostrils. This PARP had actually come from one of the ships lined up on the Cityville shoreline. The PARP meant: "HURRY UP, WE HAVE TO GO!"

Edith looked around. (Her pigeon, Gordon, didn't. He was busy looking at his feet, wondering what they were.)

"Mr Penguin?" said Edith. "Where are you?"

Then she spotted him.

He was waddling very slowly through the crowds of excited onlookers gathered to wave the shiny ship off. His Adventurer's satchel was slung across

his body as always, but he was also
lugging a great travelling trunk behind
him that was at least three times his
size and about eighteen times as heavy.

Mr Penguin was wearing armbands on his flippers, a large rubber ring around his belly and a very worried expression on his face.

"I am not sure about ANY of this…" he grumbled.

Edith rolled her eyes and refastened her bumbag firmly under her bosom.

"Now, Mr Penguin, we've been through this…" she said in a kindly, but also a no-nonsensey sort of a voice. "I *know* you don't like water and I *know* you can't swim, and I *know* you like being nice and warm and dry, but you can't ALWAYS stay at home in your igloo. You have to go out and SEE things with your eyeholes. And besides…" Edith paused to fuss with the collar of her anorak, "we all need a nice holiday – it's been nonstop adventures for some time now."

And oh boy had it!

There had been the Museum Adventure, the Mountain Adventure, and just the other day there had been the short but thrilling Mr Penguin Getting His Head Stuck Inside a Wellington Boot Adventure which had rapidly turned into the Fire Brigade Being Called Adventure, but I'll tell you all about that another time.

"And," continued Edith, "we are here to support Colin…"

At the mention of his name, Colin – Mr Penguin's right-hand spider – skittered his way wild-eyed through the crowds, past his friends, waggling a glitzy invitation in one hand and his trusty notepad in the other.

The notepad said:

COME ON, YOU PLONKERS!
WE CAN'T BE LATE!

And he darted off towards the ship.

"He's very excited, isn't he?" said Mr Penguin.

"He is," said Edith. "This is a big deal for him! Now, come on…"

Mr Penguin hoiked the trunk back up and followed as quickly as he could.

Hundreds of people had gathered to wave the *Saucy Sandra* off. Of course, it wasn't *just* the ship they were coming to see. News had spread that lots of Hollywoodland movie stars would be on board and some of the famous faces from Cityville itself! As Mr Penguin queued up to board the ship, he couldn't help but wonder who he might meet!

Eventually, a large man in a

spotless white uniform and gloves took Colin's invitation and read it aloud.

SAUCY SANDRA

Mr Herbert Chuckle and Ms Honey Crystelle
warmly invite
COLIN and his guests
MR PENGUIN, EDITH HEDGE and GORDON
aboard the Saucy Sandra to celebrate her maiden voyage.
Welcoming Party on the top deck at sunset.

He looked down at Colin, who was grinning and holding up his notepad:
HELLO I AM COLIN.

The man nodded, took Mr Penguin's trunk and politely waved the guests on board. Edith and Colin scampered up the gangplank, but Mr Penguin didn't move. His shoelace had slithered undone, and as he bent down to tie it up, he noticed something on the ground. It was a scrap of paper with some writing on it.

It said, "OR ELSE…"

Very odd… thought Mr Penguin.

Suddenly the man in the smart uniform bellowed, "ALL ABOARD!" And there was a lot of activity – ropes were untied, the large chimneys of the *Saucy Sandra* poop-pooped great clouds of grey smoke and the crowds cheered.

"HURRY UP, MR PENGUIN!" cried

WHOO

Edith from the deck.

Mr Penguin smiled, shoved the scrap of paper into his bag and hurried on board.

But of course his shoelace was still undone so he tripped, bounced on his rubber ring and went flying through the air.

OSH!

And as he hurtled headfirst towards the poop deck he thought that, yes, Edith was right – maybe he DID need a holiday…

CHAPTER TWO

HELP!

The Sunset Welcoming Party started at, well – sunset.

It had been a bit of a grumpy sort of day weather-wise, but now the winter sun had decided to pull its socks up and put on a show. The whole sky was orange and pink and gold.

The ship had set sail a few hours ago, and now it was all at sea and that tiny dot in the distance was Cityville.

Mr Penguin had to admit (whilst sliding – as politely as possible – an entire tray of fishy canapés into his mouth) that the *Saucy Sandra* was Not Bad.

Actually, it was more than that: it was Terribly Nice Indeed.

The last boat he'd been on had been the one that brought him from the Frozen South to Cityville. THAT boat had been a tiny, stinking, freezing rust bucket with more holes than an old sock. WEEKS he'd spent on it, bobbling up and down on the crashing waves, longing for some dry slippers and a hot fish finger sandwich.

He'd vowed never to set foot on a boat again, but the *Saucy Sandra* couldn't have been more different. There were no leaks anywhere for a start – the crew, all smart in their sailor suits, saw to that. They buzzed about like jaunty bees making the entire ship gleam and shine. It all looked particularly lovely now as the sun swooned below the horizon and stars started to tinkle above them.

Mr Penguin was so goggle-eyed over everything that he forgot to feel nervous. He nudged Colin, who was standing next to him combing his monobrow.

"It's so nice here," said Mr Penguin, his mouth full of a prawn puff, "that I MIGHT even feel confident enough to take my rubber ring off."

Colin whipped out his pen.

SEE, said his notepad. I TOLD YOU – NOTHING CAN POSSIBLY GO WRONG ON THIS BOAT

Next page: AT ALL.

AT ALL.

Colin was just double-underlining those two words when there was a loud BONGING noise.

A member of the crew was giving it some welly on an ornamental gong. Everyone turned, glasses in hand, to watch as a very elderly man and a tall woman took to a small stage area at the prow of the ship.

Being a Penguin Of Not Terrific Height, Mr Penguin was having to gawp at these new people through the legs of some of the other guests.

He poked Edith on the bumbag. It was a jazzy one tonight because of the party.

"Who are they?" he hissed.

"That's Mr Chuckle and his girlfriend Honey Crystelle," Edith mouthed. "Mr Chuckle is the richest

man in Cityville! He owns all the cinemas – that's why these Hollywoodland stars are here, they're his very good friends…"

Mr Penguin looked at the gang of glittering actors smiling with all their teeth and then he peered at the two people on the stage. He decided immediately that he liked Mr Chuckle. He was small, and bent over a bit like a banana, and everything about him – his face, his outfit, even his interesting choice of hairstyle – was a bit crinkled. He didn't look like a millionaire at all really – just a very jolly old man in tangerine-coloured slacks. His girlfriend didn't seem quite as jolly. She looked pinched and stern.

"Maybe she's nervous of boats too…" thought Mr Penguin aloud.

"She should have worn a rubber ring like me…"

Edith jabbed him in the armband and told him to listen.

"WELCOME! WELCOME!" Mr Chuckle cried. His voice sounded a bit like it had been run through a sieve, but his eyes twinkled. "My dear Honey and I are delighted to welcome you aboard our little boat!"

At this Honey Crystelle smiled a lipsticky smile, but it didn't quite make itself at home in her eyes.

"Now we want you to have a wonderful trip on the *Saucy Sandra* – anything you want at any time, just ask one of our excellent staff led by Captain Henry Cutlass and they will be more than happy to help you."

He wafted a hand towards where

the large man who had welcomed Mr Penguin and his chums on board was standing with some of the other crew, looking magnificently nautical in their uniforms.

Mr Chuckle briefly outlined the route the ship would be taking (south – for warmer waters) and explained that in a few days' time there would be another party – this time a very fancy one indeed to celebrate the full moon and a journey half completed.

"And…" Mr Chuckle continued, "we have the Seven Sisters Cityville Ladies Choir joining us on board with a SPECIAL GUEST, who will provide entertainment at the party and who are going to give us a sneak preview now."

At this point, seven women bedecked in the glitziest of shawls moved to the stage and Colin scuttled to join them.

The sisters – Rose, Hyacinth, Daisy, Iris, Lavender, Marigold and Gert – took their positions. Gert puffed out her squeezebox and suddenly the air filled with music – a jaunty sea shanty which made Mr Penguin tap his brogues.

Colin took a deep breath and as the ladies started to sing, he joined in.

Now, Colin's singing was *quite* unusual. He didn't make a noise, for a start. He just frantically wrote down the words to the song in his notepad and held it aloft, grinning like a magician's glamorous assistant before furiously writing the next line.

"Colin has SUCH a lovely singing voice," said Edith, fishing a clean hanky out of her bumbag and dabbing at her eyes. Mr Penguin beamed with pride: all of Colin's Tuesday night rehearsals had been for this VERY moment!

The whole sky seemed filled with the lovely music. Mr Penguin closed his eyes so his ears could listen better… but he immediately regretted it! There came a very loud grumbling sort of noise from deep below. Was it the engines? And the ship, which had been sailing so smoothly, suddenly shuddered and lurched. A great spray of icy water spattered up on deck and the party goers squealed and wobbled all over. Gordon honked like a foghorn and Edith had to steady him on her head. Several people slid into the metal railings. Mr Penguin tumbled and his rubber ring boinged straight into a crew member with a gigantic tray of mini fish finger sandwiches that flew into the air and landed on the floor all around him.

"Oops! Sorry!" said Mr Penguin with a beaky grin, as the ship continued to lurch wildly. "Let me help you!" and he bent down to pick up some of the canapés. (One found its way into his mouth BY ACCIDENT.)

"Oh… thank you," smiled the sailor – a small, flustered young man with a wispy little moustache

who straightened his cap politely.

By this point, Mr Chuckle was apologising profusely.

"Choppy waters! Thank goodness the *Saucy Sandra* is a Very Safe Ship hahahah!" he cried, then led the audience in rousing applause for Colin and the choir.

Mr Penguin joined in, but he was now feeling a bit wobbly, and not just because of the crashing waves.

Whilst everyone clapped and cheered, Mr Penguin looked down at a new scrap of paper he had found as he'd helped pick up the sandwiches.

It said:

HELP

Mr Penguin slipped the note into his bag and shuddered. He wouldn't be taking his rubber ring off just yet…

What was that noise?

It wasn't quite loud enough to wake you up properly, but you definitely heard something...

... You shifted a little in your sleep...

... Yes, there was something right there in the distance that sounded interesting, but also SUSPICIOUS...

Hmmm...

If your ears were eyes, you'd now be sleeping with one of them ever so slightly open...

CHAPTER THREE

A BIT CLAMMY ABOUT THE ARMBANDS

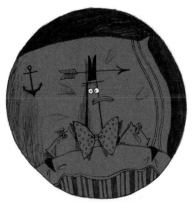

Mr Penguin worried about the rocking boat long after the ship had settled back down to its normal gentle bobbing. The party had ended with lots of jazzy fireworks and everyone had trotted off to bed excited about their first night on board and the promise of a giddy sort of day tomorrow.

Mr Penguin, Colin, Edith and Gordon's cabin was very cosy, with an enormous porthole through which the moon was dancing on the inky waves. There were two big bunks, fluffy pillows and even a little tuck box full of biscuits that the gang gobbled up as a midnight feast before brushing their teeth and turning off the light.

All was quiet, but Mr Penguin was wide awake. He sat up in bed feeling nervous, and because he was nervous, he felt hungry. He could open his trunk, but that would make a lot of noise, so he ferreted around in his satchel to see if by any chance there was another of those mini fish finger sandwiches that he could just have a soothing nibble on.

There wasn't and he knew it. He'd gobbled the last ones on the walk back to the cabin after the party. But as his flipper rummaged around in his bag it found the two scraps of paper he'd shoved in there earlier.

He hoiked them out and had a jolly good look at them through his magnifying glass. It was a very snazzy new one that Colin had bought him as a present because his old one had got spoiled in an explosion up a mountain.

There was just enough moonlight coming through the porthole to see them by.

The words OR ELSE and HELP were written, he thought, in the same handwriting, and looked to be from the same ripped-up piece of paper. Had they come from the same note? Was someone on this boat in trouble? Mr Penguin gulped. He hoped there wasn't an adventure brewing on this ship. That, combined with being completely at sea, made him feel a bit clammy about the armbands.

He turned to ask Colin what he thought about it all, but his friend was already asleep and snoring on his notepad:

ZZZZZzzzzzz.

(Double underlining meant he was in a deep sleep.)

"I'll ask him in the morning," said Mr Penguin to himself, and settled down under the covers.

The gentle sounds of Edith and

Colin both snoring (Gordon was a quiet sleeper, mainly because he slept inside a pillowcase with his legs in the air) mixed with the soft squeaking of his rubber ring around his own belly as he breathed started to make Mr Penguin drowsy.

However, just before he nodded off, he heard something outside the cabin door.

TIPTOE TIPTOE

Someone was creeping past.

Then suddenly there was a little CLONK sound, like the creeping person had stubbed their toe.

Mr Penguin stirred in his half-sleep.

What was that? he wondered.

He should go and investigate but… well, that could be dangerous and he was as keen on danger as he was on water, so he just said "Hmmmmmmmm…" suspiciously, settled down and forced himself to think nice calming thoughts about fish fingers.

Outside the cabin door, the tiptoer stood flattened against the wall in the shadows. Their eyes were wide and their heart was beating fast. They hadn't stubbed a toe – they'd bashed their elbow on a doorknob and there would be a bruise in the morning.

Had the clonking noise woken the inhabitants of the cabin?

After a few moments, the person in the shadows pressed their ear against Mr Penguin's door and listened. All that could be heard from there now was snoring.

Leaping lobsters! thought the mysterious tiptoer, that was close!

Satisfied they weren't going to be discovered, the shadowy figure continued its suspicious journey down the moonlit deck.

Tiptoe.

Tiptoe.

Tiptoe…

CHAPTER FOUR

SKULKING UNDER A SUNHAT

The next day passed by in quite a whirl of busyness.

So much so that Mr Penguin didn't find much time to be nervous about being on a boat or even tell his pals about the notes he'd found.

However, three strange things happened that were Of Concern.

It all started when Mr Penguin found himself being woken up by Colin urgently tapping on his beak with one of his feet-hands and holding up his notepad with another. The pad said:

IT'S TIME FOR

Next page:

BREAKFAST!

Well, that certainly got Mr Penguin out of bed in a jiffy, and as soon as Edith had turned Gordon out of his pillowcase and run a brush through his feathers, the gang were off to the restaurant.

And oh boy was it a breakfast to be had!

The room was packed with passengers, all tucking in and marvelling at the enormous amounts of grub on offer. There were huge cauldrons of cereal, towers of hot toast, eggs any way you wanted them, great mugs of hot chocolate overflowing with clouds of whipped cream and marshmallows, and mountains of sticky, jammy, flaky pastries that Mr Penguin considered just diving into, headfirst, with his beak open.

In the centre of the restaurant was a rather fancy sort of open kitchen at which several of the crew were standing in aprons ready to serve hot food if you wanted it. And Mr Penguin did want it. It was while he was queueing up there that the first strange thing of the day happened.

In the centre of the kitchen, Mr Chuckle was sitting merrily on a high stool wearing a chef's hat and looking like a jolly little old elf. He wasn't actually doing any of the cooking, he was just welcoming everyone and waving his walking stick happily and generally being a very cheerful, chirpy sort of person.

"GOOD MORNING, MR PENGUIN!" he hollered happily over the sizzle of some eggs the little crew member with the moustache was frying. "Would you be interested in some pancakes? Captain Cutlass here is a dab hand at making them, aren't you Henry? And he would be just delighted to rustle some up for you!"

He patted Captain Henry Cutlass on his thick arm before greeting the next person in the queue – the chief of the Cityville Police, Chief Lesby Avenue.

But when Mr Penguin peered around the pile of food already teetering on his plate to say yes he would be VERY interested in some pancakes, he was shocked to discover that the captain's mood didn't seem to match Mr Chuckle's. In fact, Captain Cutlass looked absolutely FURIOUS. So cross that it made Mr Penguin's flippers quiver and he almost dropped at least six of his croissants.

Once Captain Henry had handed over the (actually very light and fluffy) pancakes, Mr Penguin trotted back to his pals.

What could have put Captain Henry in such a bad mood? he wondered to himself. Maybe he just didn't like mornings. When there wasn't a fancy breakfast on offer, Colin wasn't usually feeling himself until he'd had three enormous coffees.

At the table, Mr Penguin tucked his napkin into his bow tie and looked over again at the captain, who was actually snarling at someone: Mr Chuckle. The millionaire hadn't noticed. He was too busy hooting at something Cityville's mayor, Nora Goldchain, was saying over a sausage sandwich.

It was then that Mr Penguin noticed Mr Chuckle's girlfriend, Honey Crystelle, sitting in the corner of the restaurant. No, not sitting:

SKULKING. She had a large sunhat on her head that shaded her head dramatically. Under the brim she was looking beadily at the captain over the top of a newspaper.

She looked very stern and was acting really oddly, but Mr Penguin couldn't quite work out what she might be thinking.

He was just about to ask Colin and Edith what they thought (you

never got much sense out of Gordon
and besides, he was too busy trying to
swallow a grapefruit whole) when all
the glamorous Hollywoodland stars
sashayed into the room with their eyes
and teeth sparkling, and took the table
next to the Adventurers.

Well, that was terribly distracting
– mainly because Edith went pink
every time they talked to her and Mr
Penguin had to cool her down by
fanning her with a crumpet. But
as he did so he kept one of
his own beady eyes very
closely on Honey
Crystelle.

CHAPTER FIVE

PIRATES?

The second strange thing happened later in the day when Mr Penguin and his chums were sitting around the swimming pool on the upper deck. And it involved pirates.

They had spent much of the morning exploring the *Saucy Sandra* with Mr Chuckle. Honey Crystelle joined them. She seemed in a jollier mood but didn't say much, just smiled a lot and wafted about in a cloud of rose perfume.

There was certainly a lot to see
– a glittering ballroom, a games room
full to the brim with every sort of board
game imaginable, a library (Edith's
eyes blinked wildly with wonder at
this), a little theatre where Colin would
be rehearsing with the choir, and then
of course the swimming pool.

Mr Chuckle had nattered
nonstop, bursting with pride. He
explained that his father and
grandfather had owned lots of ships
and he'd enjoyed being on boats ever
since he was a little boy.

(Was he mad? wondered Mr
Penguin, casually checking that his
armbands were fully inflated.)

"And now..." Mr Chuckle had
said gleefully, as he tottered into the
wheelhouse where Captain Henry

Cutlass (still looking quite grumpy) was manhandling the enormous wheel as easy as pie, "… at the grand old age of ninety-seven, I finally have my very own ship!"

Mr Penguin thought that if he were a millionaire, he wouldn't buy a ship. He'd buy something nice and solid on firm ground. But Mr Chuckle looked so giddy and pleased with himself that you couldn't help feeling happy for him.

After the tour was lunch, and after lunch Mr Penguin felt very full indeed. He'd eaten five fish finger sandwiches and a knickerbocker glory so big he'd had to stand on the table to scrape his spoon to the bottom of the glass.

He'd thought about maybe spending the afternoon floating gently in the swimming pool (it wasn't very deep), but Colin had been VERY firm about Mr Penguin leaving at least an hour between lunch and getting wet. So Mr Penguin was lying flat on his back on a sunlounger, feeling belly-full and sleepy. He tilted his hat over his eyes and listened lazily to what was going on around him. It was a bit tricky to hear everything because Colin was fast asleep on the sunlounger next to him, upside down and rustling back and forth between pages in his notepad that said:

> Zzzzzzzzzz
> and:
> RANDOM SLEEPY MUTTERINGS

Colin was thoroughly enjoying his holiday.

Mr Penguin turned his attention to what was going on by the railings.

Valentino Suave, Danton Eyre, Randolph Hunk and Manilow Kisscurl were standing with sweaters knotted raffishly around their shoulders, looking rugged and windswept and gazing at the great expanse of ocean.

"Of course," said Manilow, squinting handsomely into the middle distance, "I'm used to being on a boat. I spent a lot of time at sea when I was a pirate…"

Pirate?!

Mr Penguin opened both eyes under his hat and listened more closely.

"Well, you aren't the only one…" said Valentino, flicking a curl of hair out of his eyes in slow motion. "We all were pirates once, weren't we? Those were the good old days!"

There were murmurings of agreement from the chaps.

Mr Penguin sat up with a squeak from his rubber ring. Was he hearing things right? There were four pirates on board the *Saucy Sandra*?! A familiar nervous sort of feeling started to wobble up by his bow tie.

"Yes," said Randolph, smiling his sparkly smile, "I won an award for my role as Captain Jacob Barnacle in *Peril on the Poop-deck!*"

"Well, I won SEVERAL awards for my role as Black Spot Barry in *Davy Jones' Damp Disaster!*"

Then a bit of an argument broke out as each of the actors said (loudly) how much better he was than the others, and Mr Penguin realised that they hadn't been talking about being REAL pirates at all. Just pretend ones in movies.

"It does make you wonder though," said Danton, running a hand through his luscious locks, "how much real treasure IS out there... There must be tonnes of it buried on Mysterious Islands like in our movies. And I bet there's a load of the stuff at the bottom of the sea. Right down there – miles below..."

Mr Penguin gulped and lay very still. He didn't need reminding that he was floating along on top of some water that was probably THOUSANDS of miles deep.

He decided to dip into a conversation on the other side of him where Edith was nattering to the ladies from the Seven Sisters Choir.

Gert was busy polishing her squeezebox and tuning her triangle, but her sisters were all busy ferreting about in their handbags and showing Edith photographs of the babies they looked after at Fluffy Cuddles House, Cityville's orphanage. It was a cosy old mansion about six blocks from Mr Penguin's igloo, painted baby pink and from which came quite a strong whiff of nappy cream and talc.

"All such tiny precious cutie pies!" squeaked Miss Lavender, flipping through a book of round-faced little cherubs.

In turn, Edith plucked some photographs from her bumbag of her tiny precious cutie pie.

"I've had Gordon from when he

was an egg!" she said, the buttons on her anorak straining as she puffed her bosom out with pride. "I hatched him myself! He's a nice little thing. Flies beautifully when he gets his eyes both going in the same direction…" Mr Penguin opened his eyes to see where Gordon was. He knew his friend wasn't currently on Edith's head, which meant he was doing his own thing… which meant something weird. And sure enough, it was.

Mr Penguin watched as Gordon waddled along the edge of the swimming pool, stopping every few moments to bend his head close to the water.

"Edith?" said Mr Penguin. "What is Gordon doing?"

"Oh don't worry about him,"

cried Edith. "He's having a nice time… I think he's spotted his reflection and is listening for it to say something."

Mr Penguin had a few questions to ask about that, but just at that moment the Mayor of Cityville marched on to the deck, drawing her cardigan tightly around herself.

"I thought we were meant to be sailing south for warmer weather?" she said. "I'm blummin' freezing!"

It was actually a bit cold. If he hadn't been full of fish finger sandwiches, Mr Penguin would have nipped to his cabin to zip himself into his cagoule.

Beside him, Edith sat up, licked her finger and put it up in the air. Mr Penguin knew that was Edith's trick to tell exactly what direction they were going in.

"How strange…" she said, puzzlement making her wrinkly face wrinkle more than usual. "We don't seem to be going south at all. In fact, we seem to be going in completely the opposite direction."

Then immediately after that, something VERY dangerous happened…

CHAPTER SIX

PIGEON OVERBOARD!

The large clock on the top deck bonged 3 p.m., and despite being worried about the ship not going in the right direction, Mr Penguin brightened.

"Ooh!" he beamed. "Almost time for afternoon tea!"

Although he'd had an enormous lunch, Mr Penguin thought he could probably find room for a little nibble of something. Just a flipperful of sandwiches, a few cakes and a couple of scones with jam and cream… One

of the Seven Sisters – Hyacinth – leapt
to her feet. "Goodness!" she cried. "It's
time for our rehearsal in the theatre!
Our last one before the party tomorrow
night!" The sisters gathered themselves
with much excited twittering. There
was a lot of faffing with shawls and
handbags and cough sweets and
making sure that hankies were stuffed
securely up sleeves of cardigans.

Eventually they were ready. Gert
played a note on her squeezebox and in
perfect harmony the sisters sang:

"DO-RE-MI-FA-SO-LA-TI-
DOoooooooo! COME ON, COLIN!
IT IS TIME TO SIIIIIIIING!"

Everyone clapped while Colin
leaped up and straightened his hat. He
was ready! He skittered after the sisters
as they swished down the deck.

But then a few moments later the THIRD and DANGEROUS strange thing happened.

WHOOOSH! – the ship lurched violently. It felt like the whole ocean had shuddered. Icy spurts of water shot into the air and hammered against the ship.

Up on the top deck everyone squealed and slid all over the place.

Mr Penguin fell off his lounger and bounced towards the swimming pool, but at the last moment managed to wedge himself so he didn't fall into the water which was sloshing about wildly.

"Phew!" he said to himself, as great waves splashed over the deck.

Then Edith cried out, "GORDON! NOOOO!"

Mr Penguin snapped his head around just in time to see Gordon, blinking like nothing of interest was happening, slide smoothly across the deck, teeter a little on the edge and then – PLOP! – disappear!

"PIGEON OVERBOARD!" cried Edith, frantically. "PIGEON OVERBOARD!"

Action stations!

Everyone scrabbled to the railings. Mr Penguin looked over. Far below, bobbling about in the madly thrashing waves, was Gordon.

"Oh no! Oh no! Oh no!" yelped Mr Penguin, and he started to do his funny panicky dance, running this way and that, flapping his flippers. Behind him, Edith had found the emergency bell and began ringing it.

"Oh thank goodness!" said Mr Penguin, seeing Colin appear. "Gordon's fallen into the sea and someone needs to rescue him!"

Mad scribblings on the pad:

YES

Next page:

US.

Then Colin pushed Mr Penguin's bottom towards the railings.

"Us?" squeaked Mr Penguin. "But HOW? Gordon's all the way down there in the water and we are all the way up h—"

He stopped because Colin was grinning.

"No no no no no!" said Mr Penguin. "WE can't do it! I can't swim, remember!"

But Colin
wasn't listening. He
calmly put his pad
away, straightened
his bowler hat,
cracked what would
be his knuckles if
he had any, and
waggled his monobrow
encouragingly.

Then he delicately
shoved Mr Penguin over the edge
of the boat.

There!
There it is again!
That noise…
Just at the edge of your hearing…
but is it slightly closer now?
You only heard it for a moment,
but that's enough…
You start to fidget in your sleep…
You could go and investigate…
But that would mean leaving your
precious thing…
And you mustn't do that…
So you sleepily fidget again…
Shifting and wiggling…
Wiggling and shifting…

CHAPTER SEVEN

WHISPERINGS

If what Mr Penguin yelled next could have been heard over the sound of the wind rushing past his ears and the churning waves below him, it would have been:

"OH NO OH NO! THIS IS DREADFUL! OH MY COD FISHCAKES! OH NO OH NO OH N—"

He didn't finish that last "NO" because right before he splashed headfirst into the swirling sea, he found his rubber ring being snatched by Colin... who was now dangling from the top deck by a length of webbing spun from his bottom.

"WHAT DO I DO NOW?" squawked Mr Penguin as cold, salty water slapped his fizzog.

The *Saucy Sandra* was rocking in the water and Mr Penguin and Colin were swinging like a yo-yo that has lost its bounce. Gripping Mr Penguin firmly with one leg, Colin got out his pad. Scribblings.

CATCH GORDON
Next page:
HE'S OVER THERE
Colin licked the end of his marker pen and drew an arrow pointing to the left. Sure enough, there was a very damp Gordon bobbling about on the waves. He was blinking serenely, like falling into the ocean happened to him daily. Above them, the passengers were shouting encouragements as Colin began to shake his bottom, causing the two Adventurers to swing more extravagantly. Mr Penguin reached out his flippers.

One… SPLASH! SPLATTER!

Two… SPLASH! SPLATTER! Three times he tried to grab Gordon then eventually, with an enormous streeeeeetch – he managed it! He clamped his pigeon friend tightly under his flipper and a cheer erupted above. Gordon, sodden and bedraggled, honked loudly (which Mr Penguin took to mean "thank you"), then nestled down to sleep with his eyes open.

And as quickly as the swirling and frantic splashing of the ocean had started, it stopped. All was gentle again.

"HOW ARE WE GOING TO GET BACK ON BOARD?" shouted Mr Penguin to Colin – but Colin was, as always, one step ahead. He made the Adventurers swing even more widely, then, just as they were about to crash into the ship – KAPOW – kicked the side of the boat with his kung fu legs and all three pals hurtled through the air, sailing into an open porthole on one of the lower levels.

They tumbled across the polished floor of a long corridor before coming to a stop.

For several moments nobody moved.

Gordon was still asleep (snoring gently now) and Mr Penguin and Colin just lay flat on their backs, panting. That had been QUITE an exciting few minutes.

Eventually they stood up, and Mr Penguin adjusted his armbands.

"Well done, Colin!" he said. "Let's get Gordon back to Edith. She'll be worried…"

Colin nodded, and the chums started to stump down the corridor, leaving soggy footprints in their wake. They were just about to turn a corner when Colin halted abruptly and put a couple of legs out to stop Mr Penguin going any further.

"What—" started Mr Penguin, but Colin put a leg to his lips, pointing with another of his legs at what would be his ears if he had ears.

Mr Penguin clamped a flipper over Gordon's beak to stop him snoring so loudly and listened.

Around the corner, someone – and it sounded like Captain Henry Cutlass – was whispering.

"… tell the rest of the gang," he hissed in his low, growly voice. "A secret meeting, in the secret meeting

place at midnight. We'll get some answers from the old man – I'll make sure of it – and then our plan will be complete ready for tomorrow—"

They were interrupted by the sound of frantic running plimsolls, and someone shouting, "Captain Cutlass! Captain Cutlass! Oh, there you are!"

"What is it, Bucket?" snarled the captain, sounding (Mr Penguin thought) like he hoped he hadn't just been overheard.

"Three... Three passengers have fallen overboard, sir!" said the panting voice. Mr Penguin recognised it as belonging to Kevin Bucket – the young man with the wispy moustache who had dropped the fish finger canapés on the first night.

"OK! OK!" the captain growled.

"Tell everyone I'm on my way."

"Aye-aye, captain!" said Kevin Bucket, skedaddling back down the corridor as fast as his plimsolls would carry him.

As soon as he'd gone, Captain Cutlass whispered, "Remember – MIDNIGHT."

Then he jogged away after Kevin. Mr Penguin and Colin eyeballed each other. What on earth had they just heard? Who had the captain been talking to? And where was the secret meeting place?

Their thoughts were interrupted by the sound of a door being shut gently, like it had only been open a crack. A waft of perfume floated down the corridor. Mr Penguin knew who it belonged to: Honey Crystelle.

And then something calms you...
 A little sound that gently soothes
you back to your slumber...
 But you don't go properly back to
sleep...
 You are half awake now...
 Only dozing...
 It's like you are trying to have a nice
lie-in but your alarm clock keeps ringing...
 But you don't have an alarm clock
down here at the bottom of the ocean...
 But something keeps waking you up...
 And it's making you feel grumpy...

CHAPTER EIGHT

A NOT-QUITE-MIDNIGHT MIDNIGHT FEAST

After all the excitement, the rest of the afternoon was a bit of a wash-out.

Colin's choir practice was cancelled because Mr Chuckle fussed around insisting that the crew bring everyone a hot, sweet cup of tea. (An emergency fish finger sandwich was rustled up for Mr Penguin, who had had to eat it lying flat on the floor with his eyes closed as the memory of the crashing waves danced under his eyelids.)

Mr Penguin and the gang used Gordon's soggy session in the sea as an excuse not to go to dinner but, instead, hole up in their cabin and have a secret meeting of their own.

Colin raided the kitchens whilst Edith fussed over Gordon (who was absolutely fine, just looking slightly more odd than usual due to his feathers drying in a very blousy fashion). Now they were enjoying a Not-Quite-Midnight Midnight Feast, just the four of them.

"I knew there was something SUSPICIOUS happening on this ship," hissed Mr Penguin, fussing with his armbands. "When Colin said NOTHING CAN POSSIBLY GO WRONG, I knew that quite a lot actually could go wrong and now it has…"

He waddled up and down feeling all of a jumble – he was stuck on a boat in the middle of the ocean (that seemed not to be able to behave itself) and there was something very dangerously like an adventure brewing.

He took a deep breath and with Colin's help filled Edith (and Gordon – not that he appeared to be listening) in on the strange conversation they had overheard. She listened carefully and nodded her head and said things like "Hmmmm…" at just the right moments.

"That doesn't sound terribly good, does it…" She wrinkled her brow and tapped her head thoughtfully. "What do you think is going on?"

Colin wiped his leg-hands on a napkin and out came the pad.

PIRATES, it said.

I BET IT IS PIRATES

Next page:

IT'S ALWAYS PIRATES.

Mr Penguin gasped. "Well, I did overhear a conversation about pirates," he said, "but it was all those actors talking about them having played pirates in films…" He hoiked his rubber ring back under his armpits and pursed his beak. "Still, it was very SUSPICIOUS, if you ask me…"

"Oh yes!" beamed Edith, fanning herself with a lettuce leaf. *Peril on the Poop-deck!* – one of our favourites, isn't that right, Gordon?"

Gordon didn't say anything. He stretched out his beak, ripped a page from Edith's book and started to eat it, which caused quite a commotion.

It also made Mr Penguin remember something. He rummaged around in his bag and brought out the two ripped pieces of paper he had found, as Edith wrestled a contents page out of Gordon's mouth and smoothed it out on her bosom.

"I found one when we were getting on the ship and thought it was just some rubbish," said Mr Penguin, "but then I found the other one on the ship which means that someone here is in trouble!"

"Well isn't that a funny thing…" gasped Edith, and she rummaged in her bumbag. A selection of tools and newspaper cuttings flew out, but eventually she found what she was looking for – three pieces of ripped paper just like the scraps Mr Penguin had found.

Mr Penguin rubbed his beak thoughtfully. "What in the name of tinned salmon does it mean?" he said.

Just then two sets of footsteps crept past the cabin and the Adventurers held their breath.

After they had passed by, Colin snuck a look out of the door. Outside the cabin all was still and silent and dark.

IT'S HENRY CUTLASS

said the pad.

AND SOMEONE ELSE.

Edith rummaged down the front of her jumper for the pocket watch she kept tucked into her bra strap.

"Half past eleven!" she hissed. "I bet they are on their way to their secret meeting!"

Mr Penguin gulped. He scooped

up the scraps of paper and put them in this bag.

WE HAVE TO FOLLOW THEM, said Colin on his pad, and he disappeared out of the cabin.

Do we? thought Mr Penguin. But he knew the answer, so he just gulped again and followed Colin out into the night.

CHAPTER NINE

TIPTOE...
TIPTOE...

The sky was black outside and the sea was inky, but thankfully the moon was almost-but-not-quite full so it was throwing a weird milky light on to the deck – just enough for you to see by.

Edith was staying with Gordon, keeping a lookout through the keyhole of the cabin, so it was just Mr Penguin and Colin sneaking along the deck behind the two sinister shadows – it looked like Henry Cutlass, and maybe the sturdy frame of first mate Brenda Hoist.

The only sounds were the waves lapping against the ship far below and Mr Penguin saying, "Oh no oh no oh no oh no," under his breath, whilst his rubber ring squeaked lightly with each quivering tiptoe.

He'd been so worried about there being something happening on the ship that he'd not had a chance to think about what he would do if an adventure *was* sprung upon him. And now it had been, he didn't like it. What were these bad guys up to? he wondered, and what were they after? What happened if they caught him and Colin, and threw them overboard? How good was Colin's doggy-paddle?

Mr Penguin's bow tie started to prickle. He felt as if he and Colin were being watched. Colin didn't seem to have noticed – his monobrow was furrowed and some of his kung fu legs were flexing in case he had to KAPOW! at any moment.

Mr Penguin squinted around. He couldn't see anyone – just some lifeboats lashed to the shadowy side of the ship – but his eyes did land on something on the floor not far from him.

Another piece of paper. And another. And another. In fact, there were bits of paper everywhere.

He picked them up and read them out:

MR SKIPPER

YOU'LL BE SORRY

LAST WARNING

SHARKS

He said that last word with a squeak.

SSSSH! hissed Colin's pad.

But Mr Penguin wasn't listening.

There was one last piece of paper that was threatening to blow overboard. He waddled over to fetch it and held it up to the moonlight.

"MARINA," he read out loud.

And what happened next made Mr Penguin nearly jump out of his skin.

Because out of the darkness, a voice suddenly said:

"Yes?"

CHAPTER TEN

MARINA

Mr Penguin's heart was pounding so loudly he almost didn't hear the next thing the voice said which was, "Oh BUM!" in a very disappointed-with-itself sort of way.

"Colin!" squeaked Mr Penguin. "There's someone out here!"

Sounds of marker pen on paper.

I KNOW.

Next page:

WE ARE FOLLOWING THEM.

"No!" flustered Mr Penguin. "Someone else! They just spoke!"

The nice thing about Colin was that when he was in the detecting mood, he didn't need convincing. He just leapt into action. He jumped in front of Mr Penguin and held up his pad.

WHO'S THERE?

it said.

SHOW YOURSELF!

then:

PUDD 'EM UP! PUDD 'EM UP!

and at that he shook some of his leg-fists at the darkness.

There was a large sigh and the tarpaulin covering one of the lifeboats shifted. A face appeared.

"It's Kevin Bucket!" whispered Mr Penguin. "The cabin boy who picked up all the fish finger sandwiches!"

Kevin sighed again and said, "No it isn't…" He peeled off his wispy moustache and whipped the battered old cap from his head. Long plaited braids tumbled down.

Mr Penguin gasped. "BUT?!" he cried, his eyes almost popping out on springs.

"Leaping lobsters! Keep your voice down!" hissed Not-Kevin.

Mr Penguin clasped a flipper over his beak.

"I'm actually called Marina," continued Kevin-who-it-appeared-was-actually-called-Marina. "And I think my grampa has been kidnapped and is hidden on this ship."

Mr Penguin and Colin blinked.

"Look…" hissed Not-Kevin.

"Come in here and I'll explain everything."

CHAPTER ELEVEN

DEAR MR SKIPPER

"Oh…" said Mr Penguin. "I see…"

Well, that wasn't true at all – he couldn't even see the end of his beak in the darkness under the tarpaulin, but he understood what Marina had just said.

She had disguised herself as a cabin boy and stowed away to look for her grandfather, but as yet she hadn't had any luck.

"I think he might be right down in the engine rooms somewhere. I've been sneaking around at night looking for him, but he's nowhere to be seen!"

But whilst she had been working as a cabin boy, Marina had realised that some of the crew were Up To Something.

"I don't really know what it's about, but they have whispered conversations and secret meetings. Earlier, I think I interrupted Henry Cutlass and Brenda Hoist…"

Mr Penguin rubbed his beak. "But how did you know your grandfather was on THIS ship?" he said.

"Oh, that was easy!" said Marina. "I found a scrap of paper at his house and it said SAUCY SANDRA on it. I'll show you."

She took the cap off again and rummaged around in it.

"Oh!" she said. "It's gone!"

It was Mr Penguin's turn to rummage now – but in his bag.

"Did it look like this?" he said. He flipped the tarpaulin above their heads back a bit to let a shaft of moonlight in and showed her the scrap he'd found minutes before.

"Yes!" squeaked Marina. "It must have slipped out when I scratched my head looking for a place to hide…"

Mr Penguin got all the pieces of paper he and Edith had found and laid them out.

Marina's eyes were like saucers as he explained where he'd found them.

"It's like bits of a letter!" she said. "But it doesn't make sense…"

Colin had been watching and
listening in his beady little fashion, but
now he whipped Mr Penguin's magnifying
glass out and used it to look VERY
closely at Marina's grandfather's hat.

AHA

said the pad triumphantly, and as
Marina and Mr Penguin watched, Colin
pointed out a hole in the lining. With a
jolly good shake of the hat, several
things fell out:

An old wrinkled photograph.

A badge.

A locket.

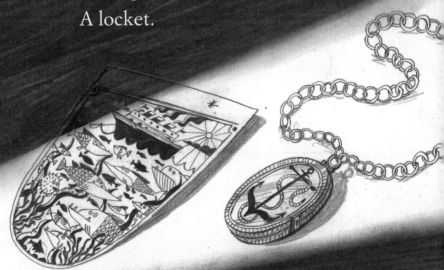

Marina picked them up and looked at them.

"These are all of my grampa's special things," she said. "Look – that's him there. When he was a little boy."

She showed Mr Penguin and Colin the photograph. It was a picture of a group of people long ago – sailors, scientists and, beaming a toothy grin, a small boy who looked just like Marina disguised as Kevin.

"And this is the badge from his uniform," she said, running a finger across the embroidered picture of a ship with a multitude of sea creatures under it. "He travelled the world with a team of explorers! They discovered all these creatures. That's what I'm hoping to be – an explorer. Or an Adventurer. OR BOTH! And this…" she picked up the locket and opened it to reveal a picture of herself, "… is me! Grampa will be sad to not have all of this with him."

"What do those numbers mean?" asked Mr Penguin, pointing to a string of figures etched inside the locket.

2 5 N 7 1 W

"Oh!" said Marina. "I don't know. It's not my birthday…"

She was distracted by Colin, who was shaking the hat like it was a snow globe. Finally some scraps of paper tumbled out.

"The missing pieces of the letter!" said Marina, and together the three new friends put the scraps together on the floor of the lifeboat. "It's like doing a jigsaw!"

But instead of revealing a nice picture of a kitten or something when they'd finished, the jigsaw showed something not very nice at all.

Marina and Mr Penguin gulped. Colin GULP-ed on his pad.

THE SAUCY SANDRA
CITYVILLE DOCKS

DEAR MR ALBERT SKIPPER

WE HAVE BEEN MORE THAN PATIENT WITH YOU FOR THE INFORMATION WE WANT. WE ARE TIRED OF WAITING. YOU HAVE IGNORED ALL OF OUR PREVIOUS LETTERS SO THIS

IS YOUR LAST WARNING. YOU'D BETTER HELP US, OR ELSE!

WE KNOW WHERE MARINA IS AND WE WILL KIDNAP HER. WE THINK THERE ARE A LOT OF SHARKS IN THE OCEAN WHO WOULD ENJOY GOBBLING HER UP.

YOU HAVE UNTIL 5 P.M. TODAY TO REPLY OR YOU'LL BE SORRY!
YOURS IMPATIENTLY,
H.C.

"Grampa IS on the boat then!" whispered Marina. "And he's in danger! But who is H.C.?"

They all thought for a moment before saying in unison:

"Henry Cutlass!"

"We KNEW he was a bad 'un, didn't we, Colin?" hissed Mr Penguin.

Just then heavy footsteps thudded by the lifeboat.

Marina pulled Mr Penguin and Colin flat.

"Pedro! Hurry up!" said a gruff voice. "It's time for the secret meeting!"

"We'll take the back stairs to the engine room!" said a snarly sort of voice.

A peek revealed it to be two more large crew members.

COME ON, said Colin's pad, as he made to follow them.

Mr Penguin's heart started beating like a big bass drum.

"Wait!" hissed Marina, eyeing Mr
Penguin in his rubber ring and
armbands. "You can't follow them
like that – you'll stand out like a
squid in a circus! You need a
disguise!"

Mr Penguin breathed a sigh of relief. "Oh, we don't have any disguises…" he said happily. "So we'll just have to wait here, nice and safe."

But Colin had other plans. He waggled his monobrow and disappeared on to the deck.

Mr Penguin and Marina couldn't see what happened next, but they heard…

KAPOW! CLONK! OOF!

CHAPTER TWELVE

A SECRET DOOR

"Are those two going to be all right?" muttered Mr Penguin, as he very carefully made his way down the creaking metal ladder into the *Saucy Sandra*'s engine room.

I ONLY CLONKED THEIR
HEADS TOGETHER A LITTLE BIT
said Colin's pad.

Well, that wasn't the full story.
Yes, there had been a little bit of head-
clonking, but Colin had also stolen
their uniforms, tied them up with some
web from his bottom and then he,
Marina and Mr Penguin had hoiked
them into the lifeboat and left them
there sleeping off their banged heads in
their vests and pants.

Mr Penguin and Colin were now
wearing the uniforms.

The Adventurers had quarrelled a
little bit over the fact that Mr Penguin
didn't want to take off his rubber ring
or his armbands. Eventually he did as
he was told and stashed his inflatables
away in his bag. They would, he had to

agree, probably draw unwanted attention when he snuck into the secret meeting.

ANYWAY

said Colin's pad,

THE RUBBER RING WILL RUIN THE LINE OF YOUR OUTFIT.

That was something Mr Penguin couldn't argue with.

Now the three pals were in the engine room right at the bottom of the *Saucy Sandra*. It was hot and shadowy, full of clangs and bangs and hisses and rumbles from all the machinery helping power the ship through the night.

"I'm sure they'll guess we are in disguise…" mumbled Mr Penguin. Just then a shout filled the air, making the Adventurers jump.

It was Henry Cutlass.

"PEDRO! MARGARET!" he yelled. "HURRY UP!"

Marina slipped into a shadowy gap to hide as Mr Penguin looked around to see who the captain was talking to.

"Who, me?" he said, realising that no one was behind him.

"Of course you, Margaret," snapped Henry. "Who else?"

Mr Penguin swallowed hard.

"I'll stay here and keep lookout," whispered Marina from her hidey-hole. "I can't come with you because I'll be recognised."

So with trembling flippers, Mr Penguin followed Colin towards Henry Cutlass.

The secret meeting was held in a

room concealed behind one of the large metal engine cylinders. The cylinder looked like all the other ones apart from a tiny metal octopus on the lower right side.

Henry Cutlass slid this to reveal a keyhole, into which he placed a large metal key.

There was a CLICK.

The entire metal cylinder swung out like a door revealing…

… yet another door inside.

Mr Penguin and Colin's eyes were like saucers – looking at it, as they were, through the taller crew members' legs.

The thick metal door was studded with rivets and spread out over it were several complicated locks. In the centre was a large metal octopus, its tentacles fanned out around it.

Henry and Brenda Hoist nodded at each other before both inserting a key into identical keyholes. They turned them.

CLUNK

Nothing.

Then suddenly the sapphire eyes of the mechanical octopus flashed, and the entire thing seemed to come to life. Tentacles twisted and turned mechanically, snaking up and down along the door's surface and unlocking various bolts and latches with loud clicks and heavy thuds.

Eventually the moving
limbs came to a stop and with a
delicate click, the door opened.

Henry and Brenda went inside, and the crew members followed.

Mr Penguin found himself glued to the floor with worry, completely unable to move.

Colin rolled his eyes, picked his friend up at the knees and carried him through the secret door.

CHAPTER THIRTEEN

ALBERT SKIPPER

The room was very small indeed, so Mr Penguin and Colin could hide at the back behind the rest of the crew members without really being noticed.

It was extremely warm in there too, and Mr Penguin wished he had one of Henry Cutlass's delicious breakfast pancakes to waft himself with. Or, of course, to eat. Mr Penguin was feeling nervous, so was starting to get belly-rumbleish.

Colin elbowed him on the
kneecap to make sure he was listening
to the captain, who was starting to
address his troops.

"All is going to plan," he growled.
"The escape boats are ready to go and
we've followed the instructions to the
last full stop. We are on course for our
devilish plan to be completed
beautifully. It's the full moon tomorrow,
and we have the Seven Sisters ready to
sing at midnight. Then…"

He paused dramatically and
grinned a wolfish grin, his large gold
tooth glinting in the lantern light. "We
will wake the sleeping—"

Mr Penguin didn't hear the next
word because his belly rumbled
extremely loudly.

"… then make our escape to the

island and the treasure will be ours!"

The crew roared and cheered with dastardly glee.

"Wake the what?" hissed Mr Penguin out of the side of his beak to Colin. "It sounded like 'cracker'. What is a sleeping cracker?" Mr Penguin's brain was immediately distracted by the thought of cheese and crackers. He could do with some of that now to calm his nerves. He slapped his own face with a flipper to make himself concentrate.

"Did you hear what they said?" asked Mr Penguin.

The pad came out.

NO.

Next page:

BECAUSE SOMEONE WON'T STOP TALKING.

And Colin underlined SOMEONE whilst looking very pointedly at Mr Penguin and put several of his what-would-be-his-hands on his what-would-be-his-hips.

Mr Penguin thought about the word he had heard AND knew the meaning of – treasure! So this crew *were* pirates!

His belly rumbled nervously again.

The cheering died down.

"The only thing left for us to find out," the captain continued, and the face that had been so pleased a moment ago was suddenly cloudy like a storm had rolled in, "is the EXACT location of the island. We know we are close. And that is where you come in, isn't it, Mr Skipper?"

At that, Brenda Hoist shifted her

large form and revealed a small, elderly man tied to a chair with rope and some jaunty nautical neckties.

Mr Penguin let out a squeak of shock.

It had to be Marina's grampa!

"This is your final chance, Mr Skipper," snarled Henry Cutlass. "We've got your precious granddaughter hidden in a box next door…"

"No he hasn't!" whispered Mr Penguin from behind his flipper.

Frantic scribblings.

WE KNOW THAT

said Colin,

BUT ALBERT DOESN'T.

"So," continued the captain, "give us the coordinates or we'll duff you both up and throw you overboard,

won't we, Brenda? The sharks WILL
be pleased with such a feast!"

At this Brenda grinned an almost
toothless grin and cracked her
knuckles. They had FISH and HIPS
tattooed on them. It should have said
CHIPS but several years ago she'd
come off worse
thumb-
wrestling a
piranha.

Albert Skipper looked at the captain and Brenda's faces. Then at their ginormous fists.

"OK... OK..." he said, sighing heavily. "The island is located here... 2 5 N 7 1 W. Just promise you'll leave little Marina alone!"

The crew ignored him, roaring with delight!

"AHA!" cheered Henry Cutlass. "The final piece we needed! Brenda – go tell the Boss. H.C. is in the wheelhouse – it's full speed ahead until morning!"

Brenda dashed off, flat-footed, and the rest of the crew followed, whooping piratically. Mr Penguin and Colin were swept along with them.

"The Boss?" said Mr Penguin, all wrinkle-browed. "H.C.?" He gasped.

"HONEY CRYSTELLE!"

As the last of the pirates left the room, Albert Skipper cried:

"Your plan will never work! I need to warn you..."

But Henry Cutlass snorted like a big proud pig and slammed the octopus door shut with a CLANG.

The tentacles performed their snaking dance across the surface, and within moments, the room was once again sealed tight.

CHAPTER FOURTEEN

A PLAN IS COBBLED TOGETHER

Back in their cabin, and still in their borrowed uniforms, Mr Penguin, Marina and Colin filled in Edith and Gordon (who was more interested in trying to listen to a glass of water) about everything that had just happened – the secret room, the coordinates for an island, and how the crew were under the command of Mr Chuckle's girlfriend, Honey Crystelle.

Edith then managed to repair the ripped-up note with sticky tape from her bumbag.

"So…" she said, "Ms Crystelle and her ruffians found out about this island, and want to get their grubby mitts on the treasure that's hidden there…" She absent-mindedly polished one of the spanners from her toolkit.

"And they needed Grampa to find it. He must have been there before," continued Marina. "But when he refused to help them – good old Grampa – they kidnapped him and have been treating him not very nicely at all until he did what they wanted!" Her cheeks went pink with crossness. "And now he's stuck in that horrible little room whilst those dreadful pirates get away with their awful plan! I'm going to go down there now and get him out!"

She leapt up, pushing back the sleeves of her jumper.

"Then I'm going to go to the kitchen and get a frying pan and wallop every single one of those pirates over the he—"

She didn't finish her sentence because Colin gently but firmly bopped her on the back of her knee, making her leg crumple.

The pad was out again:

WHOA

Next page:

WHOA

Next page:

WHOA

Next page:

HOLD YOUR HORSES, KIDDO.

YOU'LL NEVER GET
THROUGH THAT DOOR.

"Quite right, Colin," said Edith.
"That octopus lock sounds quite a
tricky little beggar if you ask me.
Wouldn't you say so, Mr Penguin?
You're being very quiet."

Well, that was true.

He was being quiet. Mainly
because he was in such a nervous fizz
that he had been piling everything left
over from the not-quite-midnight
midnight feast into his mouth like an
eating machine.

He gulped down the last beakful.

"Well," he said, "I'm wondering
two things. First of all, if Ms Crystelle
and the pirates want that treasure, why
were we all invited? Us and the film
stars and the important Cityville

people? Why not just go off on their own? I'm sure they could have found a PIRATE ship!"

Everyone said, "Hmmm…" thoughtfully.

"And the other thing," continued Mr Penguin, dreading the answer, "is… what are we going to do?"

Colin, because he knew his chum so well, clamped some of his what-would-be-his-arms on to Mr Penguin's legs, stopping him from doing his funny panicky dance.

"We need a plan!" said Marina, clamping her grampa's hat firmly on her head and jutting out her chin.

"We'll tell Chief Lesby Avenue – he's a policeman, after all," cried Mr Penguin. "Then he can arrest all the crooks and we can go home!"

"No," said Edith. "That won't work. We are facing Dangerous Foes here… If Henry Cutlass and his crew get wind of that we'll all be overboard as quick as a wink – Chief Lesby included. Also, we don't want everyone to panic."

"We're running out of time," squeaked Mr Penguin, who was already panicking. "It's past midnight, which means that the full moon is tonight. And whatever those pirates are planning happens then!"

He was right. The sky outside the porthole had changed from inky black to a hazy sort of grey, which meant dawn was just around the corner (if the ocean had corners).

Mr Penguin shoved a jam tart in his mouth and swallowed it whole.

"Yes!" Edith agreed. "We'll have to act quickly. And we'll have to be sneaky. This is what I think we should do…" She held up a finger. "One: move those unconscious sailors in here.

They won't tell us anything, I'm sure, but it'll mean two fewer dastardly devils to deal with. Besides, we need to keep hold of their uniforms."

Another finger went up in the air. It looked quite rude, but Mr Penguin decided now wasn't the time to say anything about that.

"Two: the person we need to tell about this is Mr Chuckle. That's your job, Mr Penguin and Colin. He'll be able to get this ship to turn around and get the pirates AND Honey Crystelle arrested back in Cityville. He might not believe you – Ms Crystelle IS his girlfriend after all – but you'll have to try. Also, as you are disguised as sailors, try to find out more about what Henry and Honey have planned for tonight…"

Colin grinned. He lived for this sort of thing. Mr Penguin didn't, so he just gulped.

"Three: meanwhile, I'm going to try and get that octopus door open!"

Edith tapped her bumbag and her tools jangled.

"What about me?" said Marina. "I want to help too! I mean, I have to swab the decks – that's my morning job and if I don't do it, the captain will know something is up…"

"Ah!" said Edith. "You can do that AND help – you can be my lookout. If anyone tries to get down to the engine room, clang your bucket!"

"And what if that doesn't stop them?"

HIT THEM OVER THE HEAD WITH YOUR MOP

said Colin's pad.

Marina grinned and leapt up.

"Come on then!" she cried.
"Let's go – it's already morning!"

The Adventurers scrambled to
their feet.

Mr Penguin wanted to ask if
"having a nice breakfast" was part of
Edith's plan, but it didn't seem to be,
so he just straightened his sailor's hat
and followed his friends out of the
cabin.

CHAPTER FIFTEEN

UNDER COVER

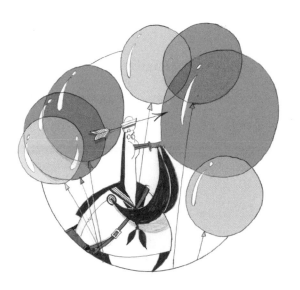

Finding and warning Mr Chuckle of the dastardly plan going on right under his nose turned out to be jolly difficult. From the moment the sun rose, the ship was a hive of activity getting ready for the full moon party that night.

Mr Chuckle wasn't in his usual spot at breakfast, and because they were still disguised as crew members, Mr Penguin and Colin didn't get to enjoy any of the nice food. Although, he thought as he handed over half a grapefruit to Manilow Kisscurl, there didn't seem to be anywhere near as much food this morning. I hope we aren't running out of grub! thought Mr Penguin with a belly rumble.

The rest of the day passed busily with Henry Cutlass and Brenda Hoist barking out instructions, and the crew following them quick smart. It wasn't easy as the ship was going full speed.

Standing on deck, you had to brace yourself against the stinging wind that slapped you about the face like you'd been walloped with a large wet fish.

Mr Penguin and Colin ended up folding napkins, blowing up balloons and putting up string after string of fairy lights on the poop deck, all the while keeping their peepers peeled for Mr Chuckle so they could dash over to him and warn him that he needed to turn the ship around. But the millionaire was nowhere to be seen.

"Where can he be?" said Mr Penguin as he untangled his legs from a string of lights for the fourteenth time. "You don't think he's been fed to the – GULP – sharks, do you?"

Colin wasn't sure, but he was like a coiled spring and kept flexing his kung fu kicking legs in case they were needed. Eventually, he took matters into his own sort-of-hands and scuttled off, returning two minutes later with a tea tray. He walked straight up to Henry Cutlass and tapped him on the ankle.

"What is it, Pedro?" snarled the captain.

Colin held up his pad:
TEA FOR
MR CHUCKLE.
Next page:
WHERE IS HE?
"He's in his
office getting ready

for the party," snapped Henry. "Actually, I'LL take that to him."

He snatched the tray from Colin and stomped down the deck to Mr Chuckle's office.

Colin scuttled back.

"Well done, Colin!" Mr Penguin said. "Now we know where to find him. What do we do now?"

WE WAIT

said Colin, and oh boy did they.

They hung around near the office for hours. Mr Penguin must have polished every piece of brass nearby a thousand times. They missed afternoon tea AND dinner, and around them the sun set and the full moon rose high into the sky.

"It's too late!" Mr Penguin whispered, waddling back and forth in a flap. "The party starts any moment and whatever is going to happen is going to happen! Oh no! Oh no! Oh no! Oh—"

Colin schlonked his pal on the brogue with his pad and pointed.

LOOK

Mr Penguin peeked from behind his flippers.

The office door was opening and out slipped Honey Crystelle in a cloud of rose perfume and looking very glamorous in a sparkly frock. She tottered down the deck on her very high heels and disappeared down a corridor.

The office door swung almost-but-not-quite shut behind her.

GO!

instructed Colin's pad, but Mr

Penguin hardly had time to read it before – KAPOW! – Colin had walloped him on the bottom and the two friends tumbled at full speed into Mr Chuckle's office.

CHAPTER SIXTEEN

A WARNING!

The Adventurers came to an untidy stop in the centre of the room, leapt to their feet and dusted themselves off.

The office wasn't terribly big and was lit by a single lamp perched on a mahogany desk that took up most of the room.

It wasn't quite what Mr Penguin expected. For a millionaire, he thought, Mr Chuckle's office was very plain. There was nothing on the walls and just a large open box on the floor. In the box, Mr Penguin saw lots of photos of Mr Chuckle grinning proudly next to famous people outside his cinemas or at parties.

Taking up a large portion of the desk – behind some half-drunk cups of tea, a little brass plaque with Mr Chuckle's name on it and some sweet wrappers – was a perfect model of the *Saucy Sandra*. There were even little model people standing on the top deck. It was wonderful and Mr Penguin would really have liked a very close look at it, but one glance from Colin told him that now wasn't the time.

"Everything OK, Margaret?" said
a voice.

Mr Penguin jumped and spun
around. Then he relaxed. It was only
Mr Chuckle. He'd been
straightening his
bow tie, unseen,
in the mirror
behind them.
He hobbled

back to the desk and sat himself in the comfortable chair behind it.

Mr Penguin stood glued to the floor with his mouth open until Colin prodded him.

"N-no…" stammered Mr Penguin. "It's not Margaret Spanner… It's me – Mr Penguin!"

He lifted Margaret's sailor's hat off his head to reveal himself then plonked it back again.

"I am in disguise!"

"Oh!" gasped Mr Chuckle, then his wrinkly face crinkled in a smile. "So it is you! Now what can I do for you, Mr Penguin? Why are you dressed as Margaret Spanner?"

Colin nodded encouragingly, so Mr Penguin took a deep breath and launched into his tale. He told Mr

Chuckle all about the scraps of paper and how he'd been sure something strange was going on. He explained about Marina and the ripped-up note they'd put together, about H.C. and the secret meeting, how the ship was overrun with pirates, how Marina's grandfather was hidden behind a locked octopus door, and how something dreadful was being planned at midnight.

Then he took another deep breath.

"And…" he said, "I'm afraid Henry Cutlass isn't the only person behind it. I… I think everything has been planned by your girlfriend – Honey Crystelle!"

There was a moment of silence as Mr Chuckle took this in.

"Oh!" said Mr Chuckle quietly. "Oh dear oh dear oh dear…"

Mr Penguin didn't know what to do so he looked at Colin, who was frowning, lost deep in thought.

Mr Penguin stumbled on. "Yes, I think it is your girlfriend…" he said. "Well – I know it is… You see…"

Here Colin edged closer to his friend and tapped him on the ankle. Mr Penguin pushed on with what he was saying, taking the sticky-taped letter out of his bag and holding it up.

"… the letter is signed H.C., which we thought meant 'Henry Cutlass' until—"

Again, Colin tapped Mr Penguin on the ankle, but more urgently this time. Mr Penguin glanced down to see his spidery friend looking pointedly towards the model ship on Mr Chuckle's desk. What in the name of trout paste on crumpets was Colin trying to tell him?

Mr Penguin shook his head, and carried on: "Yes, we thought H.C. was Henry, until we heard Henry himself say 'THE BOSS' and we thought, 'Who else could H.C. be if it isn't Henry?' And then we realised it must be Honey Crystelle because there's no one else on this ship with the initials H.C...."

Colin walloped Mr Penguin's ankle with his pen. When Mr Penguin looked down, he saw his friend GLARING at him and holding up his pad, on which was a thick arrow pointing at the model boat.

Mr Penguin looked again at the boat. What did that have to do with H.C.?

His eyes trailed over the mess of papers and mugs and sweet wrappers, trying to think what Colin was telling him. Now really wasn't the time for Colin to be after a cough drop!

"Um," said Mr Penguin, "I was saying that she's the only other person with the initials H.C...."

Then he spotted it.

What Colin had been pointing at.

It wasn't the model boat.

It was the brass name plaque sitting quietly on the untidy desk.

Mr Penguin gasped as he read the words engraved on it.

"Except..." he whispered.

"ME!" snarled the man behind the desk.

CHAPTER SEVENTEEN

WE ARE IN DANGER

If there was ever a moment Mr Penguin needed a fish finger sandwich, it was now.

But even if he had had one tucked helpfully in his satchel, he wouldn't have been able to whip it out. His flippers started to quiver like a nervous jelly.

They had been duped! Caught out! Slapped about by a collection of red herrings!

Manic laughter filled the cabin office, much louder and scarier than Mr Penguin ever would have imagined could have come from such a tiny old man, as Herbert Chuckle rocked with glee.

"You seriously believe that bunch of dunderheads could have put this plan, my GENIUS plan, together by themselves?" he hooted, dabbing at his eyes with a monogrammed hanky. "It was all me! I did the hunting through piles of library books! I found the information about the island! I found out about Albert Skipper! Me! Me! All me!"

The look on Mr Chuckle's face changed from glee to deadly seriousness.

"Of course, I needed that band

of pirates for their muscles and nautical know-how," he growled. "But their tiny brains are no match for mine! I might be old, but I'm as sharp as a very sharp pin! My only mistake was agreeing to let Colin join the Seven Sisters Choir. I should have known the pair of you would try to meddle in my scheme. But no matter. You'll never get your flippers on my treasure!"

Mr Penguin and Colin had been slowly backing away from the desk and were now backed against the far wall of the office.

"But... but..." stammered Mr Penguin, suddenly finding his voice (even though it came out a bit squeakily). "I don't understand. You've got heaps and heaps of money – why do you want to find buried treasure?"

A wide grin crept across Mr Chuckle's wrinkled face. "Ha!" he snorted. "You see, there we go – another inferior brain! There are many types of treasure, Mr Penguin..."

He took a pocket watch out from under his jacket and checked the time.

"But as the party is about to begin, I believe your time is running out!"

Well, Mr Penguin didn't understand a word of that. How could piles of gold coins and diamonds not be treasure? Unless the coins were made out of chocolate? But then why put together this dastardly plan for some chocolate (nice as chocolate was)? With all of Mr Chuckle's money, surely he could buy as many chocolate coins as he wanted?

Mr Penguin's belly rumbled.

Colin slid his pad into Mr Penguin's field of vision.

It said:

YOU ARE THINKING ABOUT CHOCOLATE COINS, AREN'T YOU?

Not taking his eyes off Mr Chuckle, Mr Penguin nodded, not in the least bit surprised that his best pal had read his mind.

WELL STOP IT

said the pad.

Next page:

WE ARE IN DANGER.

DANGER was underlined several times, so he was serious. Mr Penguin concentrated.

"What do you mean?" he said. "What's going to happen?"

Mr Chuckle laughed again. "You think that I'd tell you that? But I'll give you a clue…"

He picked up the model of the *Saucy Sandra* and threw it to the floor, smashing it into pieces.

"Of course," he giggled, "I'll have escaped long before that happens. But YOU won't. None of you will!"

Whether it was a sudden flash of bravery, or just the need to get out of the office and find a calming fish finger sandwich, Mr Penguin wasn't sure, but he found himself bristling.

"WE WILL!" he shouted. "WE ARE GOING TO TELL EVERYONE WHAT YOU ARE UP TO THEN YOU'LL BE SORRY! CHIEF LESBY AVENUE WILL ARREST YOU!"

And before Mr Chuckle could

answer, Mr Penguin and Colin scampered across the office to the door. But as they reached for the handle, the door burst open and BASH!, clonked SMACK! BANG! right into the Adventurers, very hard indeed.

"OUCH!" cried Mr Penguin, flattened behind the door, then everything went foggy and black.

CHAPTER EIGHTEEN

A DEAFENING ROAR

Mr Penguin slowly opened his eyes.

Oof! His head was spinning and his beak was sore. It felt all crinkled up like a bruised banana.

"What happened?" he groaned as his eyes became accustomed to the gloom. His beak was definitely Not In A Good Way because his voice came out all bunged-up and muffled.

He realised that he was still in Mr Chuckle's office, but the millionaire had left and the lamp had been turned off. He tried to move but found that he was knotted up with a thick rope. Colin was beside him.

There was some rustling as Colin managed to squeeze a few of his arm-legs out from the tightly bound coils to hold up his pad.

HENRY CUTLASS CAME IN AND THE DOOR KNOCKED YOU OUT

More rustlings.

AND THEN HE TIED US

BOTH UP AND LEFT WITH

"Mr Chuckle…" said Mr Penguin.

Colin turned the page, crossed out MR CHUCKLE and wrote YES instead.

Sounds of a party in full swing were floating in from outside. There was excited chattering and jazzy music from a gramophone, and the hearty booming laugh of Mr Chuckle – quite different from his manic cackling in the office not that long ago.

How clever Mr Chuckle is, thought Mr Penguin, foggily, to be able to pretend to be such a nice, jolly old man, whilst all the time wickedly plotting something dastardly. All the people on deck – the Seven Sisters, the film stars, the mayor and the police chief – had no idea that there was anything dreadful going on.

Thinking about the Seven Sisters and the film stars made Mr Penguin wrinkle his brow. Without knowing it, they were all part of Mr Chuckle's plan, but what part were they going to play? What did seven fluffy old ladies and some glamorous actors have to do with buried treasure? Whatever it was, it was almost midnight and they had to act fast. Or, thought Mr Penguin hopefully, someone else might take charge so he could go and have a nice lie-down in the safety of his travelling trunk.

He knew that wouldn't happen though, so he sighed.

"Colin," he said. "We need to get out of this office. Can you KAPOW us out of these ropes with your kung fu kicking legs?"

Colin tried his hardest but no – he was too tightly tied up.

Mr Penguin struggled up (bringing Colin with him) and started to do his panicky dance, running back and forth across the office.

Suddenly Colin GASPed on his pad!

Scribblings.

MR PENGUIN, RUN AT THE DOOR.

Next page:

VERY FAST

Mr Penguin did as he was told (for once) but half-heartedly.

FASTER THAN THAT, YOU PLONKER

said the pad.

"But my poorly beak!" said Mr Penguin, but Colin just rolled his eyes.

As Mr Penguin waddled as fast as he could across the room, Colin punched the two arm-legs that were free like a piston, building up energy.

Closing in on the door, Mr Penguin squeezed his eyes shut…

KAPOW!

Colin punched a Mr-Penguin-and-Colin-shaped hole right through the door and the two Adventurers skidded and tumbled across the deck.

They boinged to a halt at the far end of the boat, just in time to hear Mr Chuckle inviting the Seven Sisters Choir on to the stage.

"Such a shame our special guest Colin is unwell this evening," he lied.

"But your performance
will still be so beautiful."

There was a lot of
polite applause, and as
the clock struck
midnight, under the light of
the full moon, the Seven Sisters
started to sing.

It was oddly otherworldly, but Mr
Penguin and Colin hardly got a chance
to appreciate it because as soon as the
first musical notes filled the air, the sea
started to churn and bubble. The *Saucy
Sandra* started to lurch high in the air
and crash back into the water. Thick
storm clouds filled the sky and poured
with rain.

And from below the ship,
under the thrashing waves, came a
deafening ROAR.

There's no mistaking it now.

The sound you thought you'd been hearing is there as clear as anything, right above you.

A sweet, lovely sound but one that makes it impossible to continue your slumber.

It calls to you, telling you not in words, but in some strange dreamy way to leave the safety of the deep, and the precious treasure you've been guarding all these years, and swim to the surface to hear more.

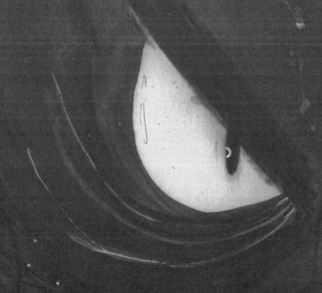

But you don't want to.
You want to carry on sleeping and
guarding, but you can't.

You suddenly feel very cross.
How DARE you be woken up!

Despite yourself, you find your
eyes opening.

Your gigantic limbs untangle and
begin propelling you up to the surface.

You ROAR ferociously because
you are now very, VERY angry.

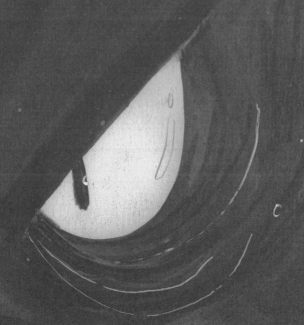

CHAPTER NINETEEN

DEFINITELY NOT A CRACKER

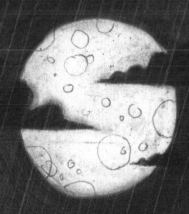

Lots of things happened almost at once.

Freezing rain hammered down upon the *Saucy Sandra* as it was thrown about on the waves. At the prow of the ship, the party guests started to panic as they were jostled about, their best party clothes now soaked in the sudden storm.

"KEEP SINGING!" shouted Mr Chuckle over the noise. His usual kindly, slightly dotty side had vanished, replaced with his mean and snarly voice.

The Seven Sisters, who, like the rest of the passengers, had no idea what was happening, or that Mr Chuckle was a Thoroughly Bad Egg, tried to do as he asked. They were troopers and kept singing their jaunty sea shanty even as bucketfuls of water thundered over them from both the sea and the sky.

The pirate crew leapt into action – not helping anyone, but untying a speedboat that had been disguised as a lifeboat under some tarpaulin.

At the other end of the *Saucy Sandra*, Mr Penguin and Colin were

still lashed together. They
rolled helplessly towards
the edge of the boat, the
inky waves waiting
menacingly far below
them.

The boat
lurched again,
throwing them
over the side…
only to find
themselves
grabbed and
hoiked back to safety.

Mr Penguin opened his eyes (that
had been absolutely and completely
squeezed shut) to see Edith, Gordon
and Marina beside them. Edith had
saved them from flying overboard, and
she now set to work freeing them. Into

her bumbag she dived, pulling out a strong pair of scissors and starting to cut through their ropes.

"Oh! Thank goodness!" said Mr Penguin. He was excited for his flippers to be free, so he could look for anything tasty in his bag that might calm his tattered nerves.

Then he realised that Marina's grampa, Albert, was nowhere to be seen. Shouting over the noise of the storm and the singing, Mr Penguin asked where he was.

"We couldn't unlock the octopus door!" cried Marina. "Edith kept trying but Honey Crystelle kept disturbing us! She's definitely up to something!"

"MAYBE!" hollered Mr Penguin. "But it isn't what you think!"

And as chaos happened around

them, and Edith swapped to her gardening shears and continued to work on the thicker ropes, Mr Penguin and Colin quickly filled their pals in on what had happened in the office.

"But Mr Chuckle is—" said Edith.

Mr Penguin finished her sentence: "Such a nice jolly old man!"

Finally, Edith cut through the last rope and Mr Penguin and Colin were free. "Right!" she said, all business. "We need to get cracking if we have any hope of this ship not finding its way to the bottom of the ocean!"

She started to run towards the prow.

"BUT WHAT IS ACTUALLY HAPPENING?" shouted Mr Penguin, following her as fast as his little penguin-y legs could manage.

"WE DON'T KNOW WHAT MR CHUCKLE'S PLAN IS!"

Edith stopped.

"We do!" she shouted. "Albert told us through the keyhole – he explained all about the full moon, midnight, the Seven Sisters singing! They are all the ingredients you need—"

"Yes?" interrupted Mr Penguin, terrified, but also (despite himself) eager to know more. "It's to 'wake the cracker' or something? That's what Henry Cutlass said at the secret meeting."

"No!" said Edith, the specs on their chain flying about in the storm. "Not to 'wake the cracker', Mr Penguin. To wake a KRAKEN!"

At the party end of the boat, someone cried out in horror.

"I DON'T KNOW WHAT THAT MEANS!" yelped Mr Penguin, but Colin did.

He scribbled on his pad and held it up.

A KRAKEN IS

Next page:

A GIGANTIC SEA MONSTER!

And at that exact moment, an enormous tentacle burst through the waves and crashed down on the deck of the *Saucy Sandra*, right beside Mr Penguin's trembling brogues.

CHAPTER TWENTY

GREAT RUBBERY THINGS ALL OVER THE PLACE

Tentacles.

Giant tentacles everywhere.

The great rubbery things burst through the waves and wrapped themselves tightly around the *Saucy Sandra*, splintering the wooden decks and crumpling metal like it was paper.

The ship lurched to the side and Mr Penguin, shocked by what was happening around him, started to slide towards the freezing sea again.

Colin snapped to attention

and, with some webbing spun at the speed of light from his bottom, caught his friend and hurled him back on board.

"Thank you!" panted Mr Penguin.

Colin nodded curtly – he hated fuss.

Mr Penguin looked about. It was absolute pandemonium. The ship was being tossed about like pizza dough and the guests were running this way and that, avoiding the squirming tentacles.

"Look!" cried Edith, holding Gordon firmly to her head as she skidded on the soaking wet floor. "Chuckle! He's getting away!"

Sure enough, there was Henry Cutlass helping Honey Crystelle and Herbert Chuckle, who now had a large bag slung across his back, into the speedboat as it was lowered into the sea.

The rest of the crew were now untying a second, larger speedboat – a difficult task whilst being attacked by a monster.

"The escape boats!" gasped Marina.

Edith's face was set and determined. "Marina, Mr Penguin, Colin – you'd better follow Chuckle!" she said.

Marina nodded, grabbed Mr Penguin and began running down the deck towards the thick of the action. Colin scuttled along beside them.

"Or! Or!" shouted Mr Penguin. "We could go to our cabin and hide?" He smiled his best winning smile, hoping to convince his pals of his much better plan.

Edith rolled her eyes. "Go!" she

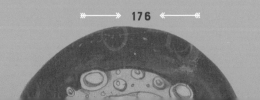

cried firmly. "Chuckle's getting away!"

"But... but... but..." called Mr Penguin. "What about you, Edith?"

Edith grinned. "Don't you worry about me, chum!" she cried, a giddy look in her eyes. "We've got plenty to be getting on with here, haven't we, Gord?"

Gordon blinked.

Edith unclasped her bumbag. "We'll be fine, Mr Penguin!" She twirled it wildly above her head, charged at full speed towards the nearest tentacle and began walloping it with all her might.

Mr Penguin's attention was grabbed by what his feet were doing. Or rather, what they were being made to do by Marina, who was dragging him towards the prow of the ship. They stopped on the very lip of the poop deck. Below them, the sea splashed wildly as tentacles unfurled monstrously from the deep.

Mr Chuckle's speedboat was now weaving away from the *Saucy Sandra* at high speed.

Mr Penguin's belly was doing somersaults. He knew what was coming next.

"We are going to jump, aren't we?" he said with a sigh. He glanced at Colin, who grinned and grabbed Marina's hand and Mr Penguin's flipper.

Then they leaped.

"I'M JUST VERY CONCERNED," cried Mr Penguin as he plummeted towards the icy sea, "THAT YOU'VE FORGOTTEN THAT I CAN'T ACTUALLY SWIM..."

CHAPTER TWENTY-ONE

FROM THE DEPTHS

Mr Penguin didn't like water at the best of times, but as it sloshed around him, trying with all its might to drown him (or worse, ruin his satchel), he decided that he loathed it.

"Colin!" he yelped, spitting out beakfuls of salty water. "My rubber ring! In my bag!"

Colin, who was bobbling about on the waves like a rubber duck in a bubble bath, saluted and dived under the water. In a matter of seconds he had retrieved and inflated the ring, and plonked Mr Penguin into it.

Mr Penguin caught his breath just in time for Marina, who was a wonderful swimmer, to point at the dark horizon and the speedboat disappearing from view.

"Over there! Mr Chuckle's heading that way!" she cried. "That must be where the island is!"

And she set off, swimming as quickly as she could.

"I'll never be able to paddle THAT speedily!" said Mr Penguin, but he needn't have worried – Colin had a plan. As quick as a flash, Colin grabbed hold of Mr Penguin's rubber ring with a couple of his leg-hands, and the rest of his limbs powered through the water like a motor engine.

It wasn't long before Mr Chuckle's speedboat was in view again, and the Adventurers slowed down for a conflab. Behind them the kraken's tentacles were still snaking out of the ocean, attacking the *Saucy Sandra*, and all the fairy lights Mr Penguin and Colin had put up earlier were fizzing and sparking and sputtering out. Mr Penguin tutted. All that climbing up and down ladders in the wind to put them up, for nothing!

"I don't understand," panted Marina, treading water. "There IS no island!"

But the words were hardly out of

her mouth when all three pals watched, gobsmacked, as something started to emerge from the water in front of them.

"Oh no!" sighed Mr Penguin. "Not *another* kraken!"

One had been quite enough for him. At least for today.

But Colin's pad (which was miraculously dry – Mr Penguin wanted to ask how that was possible, but perhaps now wasn't the moment) was out and he was scribbling away frantically.

IT'S THE ISLAND!

And it was.

Out of the depths emerged a huge, dark shape.

It wasn't what Mr Penguin had imagined the island would look like at all. He'd thought it would be all lush green leaves and sandy beaches, good for having a nice lie-down in the sunshine, but this was very different indeed.

There was not single palm tree growing on it. It was just a great hunk of rock, a bit like a gigantic curled seashell.

It finished rising from the waves. Every time the lightning crackled it stood silhouetted against the sky.

Mr Chuckle's speedboat slowed down beside a gnarled clump of coral on the right-hand side, and dark figures jumped out and disappeared through a concealed entrance.

"Quick!" shouted Marina over a rumble of thunder (and, coincidentally, over a rumble of nervous hunger from Mr Penguin's belly). "We need to follow them!"

Mr Penguin couldn't help but wonder about the word "need" in that sentence.

But what else could they do? They were stuck between two not very jolly situations. They could go back to a ship that was being attacked by a sea monster or follow a dangerous group of lunatics into an island that had just bobbed up from the bottom of the sea.

He didn't want to do either. He wanted to just stay there, bobbling about in his rubber ring until everything blew over and he could somehow get back to Cityville and his nice, safe igloo.

But Colin's legs powered up again like a motor engine, and Mr Penguin found that he was being propelled very quickly towards the island, inside which those crooks were no doubt up to something mad and very dangerous.

CHAPTER TWENTY-TWO

LIKE AN ICEBERG

"We have to be very quiet," hissed Marina. Despite the nerve-racking situation the Adventurers were in, she was as cool as a cucumber.

Mr Penguin nodded. He was too nervous to do anything else.

The three pals were on the island. They'd clambered soggily up the rocks and behind the clump of coral they had found the dark entrance to a cave.

They slipped inside and discovered a long spiralling passageway. Somewhere far ahead of them the low rumble of voices could be heard. It seemed to be Mr Chuckle and Henry Cutlass, and from the sound of it they were arguing, but they were too far underground to hear clearly.

"This island must be like an iceberg," whispered Marina as she wrung out some water from her braids, ready to crack on with the adventure at hand. "There's a lot more of it under the sea than on top of it. Whatever treasure Mr Chuckle is after must be hidden deep below the surface. Come on – let's go!"

And she started to creep as quietly as possible down the passage. Colin scampered after her.

Mr Penguin reluctantly followed. He tried his hardest to not make any noise, but every few steps Marina or Colin turned to SSH! him because his rubber ring was squeaking and his soggy brogues were squelching along the ground. His beak was still smarting from its run-in with the office door, so he was also snuffling like a piglet with a cold. As he tiptoed behind his chums, he felt it gingerly with his flippers and groaned. It was all crumpled out of shape.

The tunnel snaked steeply down into the strange rocky island.

It was a difficult journey because the ground was not only uneven, but also covered with stinky, slimy seaweed that slithered and shifted in a cold breeze that rustled eerily through the tunnel.

The three Adventurers trudged on, and eventually the voices of Mr Chuckle and Henry Cutlass in front of them became louder.

"Well, we're here!" snarled Henry. "Where's this treasure you've promised me?"

A blue-green glow was now lighting the tunnel, which opened up into a chamber at the very base of the island – who knows how deep below the surface of the sea outside.

Marina, Mr Penguin and Colin got a shuffle on and scampered out of the corridor. They edged along a shadowy, narrow walkway that circled

part of the cave, at the end of
which was another flight of steps
cut roughly from the rock and leading
down to the chamber. The Adventurers
hid behind one of the enormous
stalagmites and watched beadily.

Beneath them, the two men were
bickering, utterly clueless that they were
being watched.

"Where's Honey?" mouthed Mr
Penguin. He was worried the glamorous
but sneaky crook was going to leap
out at any moment, catch
them and feed them to
some sharks or the kraken.
Marina shrugged.
Beside her Colin remained
on High Alert, taking in
their new surroundings
with his bright eyes and

twitching monobrow.

It was a gigantic space with seaweed-covered rocky walls. From the roof, amongst knife-sharp stalactites, a great twisted piece of coral hung down like a strange chandelier. Dotted about on its bleached branches were blue shapes which lit up the entire chamber with a spooky, ghostly glow.

From what Mr Penguin could see (and that wasn't a lot from between his flippers) there wasn't a treasure chest overflowing with jewels or even a single gold coin anywhere.

"Shut up!" snapped Mr Chuckle, hobbling about in a tizz. "I'm looking for something… Aha! There it is!"

From their hiding place, the

Adventurers saw the old man brushing seaweed from a large shell sticking out from the slimy wall. He twisted it sharply to the right like he was turning on a tap, and moments later a grinding sound echoed about the space as the wall split in two and parted like a pair of lace curtains.

Mr Penguin momentarily forgot to be nervous as he watched with gigantic eyes.

Mr Chuckle snorted with pride.

"Here it is!" he gasped, awestruck. "What I've been searching for all these years! Something more precious than gold!"

CHAPTER TWENTY-THREE

POSEIDON'S LAIR

"COR!" breathed Mr Penguin. Colin immediately held up his pad. He'd sensed something shocking was about to happen so had prepared it ready:

FOR GOODNESS' SAKE, MR PENGUIN

Next page:

REMEMBER TO BE QUIET.

But what now appeared from behind the rock and seaweed curtain certainly deserved a "COR!"

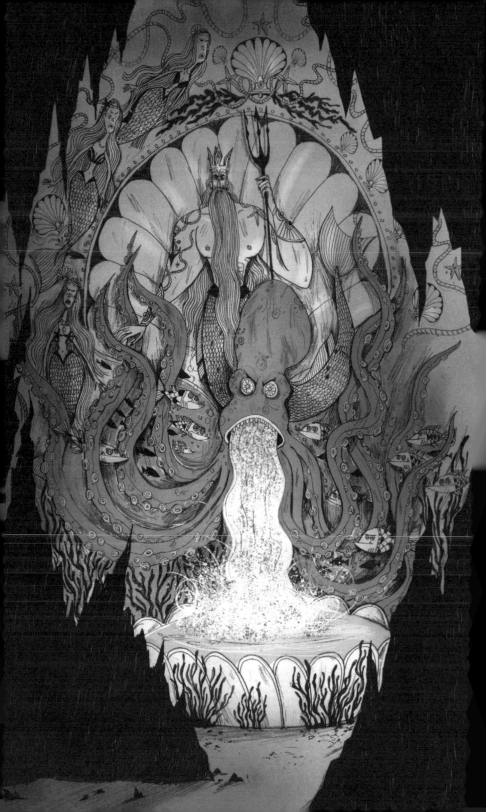

It was both beautiful and sinister. Filling the far corner of the underground lair was an absolutely enormous carving. Amongst twisting stone sea plants and all manner of fish (their scales picked out with twinkling sapphires) were mermaids, glistening in the flickering light which made them look almost alive. They were swimming around a gigantic stone kraken with snaking tentacles, mean eyes and a mouth jam-packed with sharp, pointy teeth. In the centre of the sculpture was the sea king with his long beard, scaly fish tail and trident. (Colin explained on his pad that his name was Poseidon, and that you said it like this: Po-sigh-den. Mr Penguin thought that was jolly useful information.)

As the two crooks and three Adventurers watched, the sea king's eyelids flickered open mechanically, revealing ruby eyes, and with another grinding sound his carved hand shifted like a lever. The stone kraken's mouth opened and out gushed a stream of crystal-clear water.

Mr Penguin found it rather tricky to hear everything that was being said over the noise of the water, so he leaned forward from his hiding place and held a flipper up to his ear.

The pirate captain shook his head angrily. "Where's the treasure chest?" he snarled. "You promised me a treasure chest!"

"I did no such thing!" snapped the elderly millionaire. "I said I was looking for something buried on an island and I needed your help. All I said was that it was a very precious treasure, and this is it!"

Henry Cutlass made some livid spluttering noises and Mr Penguin leaned further forward so he could listen more closely. He steadied himself with one flipper against the slippery rock beside him.

Down below, Mr Chuckle grinned a devilish grin, his face puckered like an evil prune.

"Don't you see?" he said. "I've found the Fountain of Youth!"

And it was at precisely that moment that Mr Penguin's grip slipped. He tumbled bum-over-beak from his hiding place and skidded to a halt right beside the millionaire's feet.

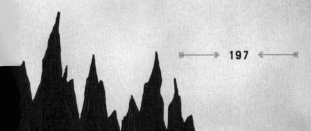

CHAPTER TWENTY-FOUR

NEWS FROM THE SS. *SNOOPING SAILOR*

Mr Chuckle had been strutting around in a highly gloating manner, but now, as a slightly soggy penguin rolled to a stop in front of him, the smile was wiped off his face.

"YOU?" he spat. "But you should have been gobbled up by that monster like the rest of them! What are you doing here?"

Mr Penguin sat up.

"Oh!" he said nervously. "It's actually rather a long story—"

But before he could continue, Marina and Colin leapt out from their hidey-hole and ran down the steps.

Marina cried, "We've come to stop you and your awful plan!"

Mr Chuckle laughed. "But you don't even know what it is!"

Well, that was true.

"Shall I tell you?" said Mr Chuckle, the gloating manner back in full force now. "Then you'll be in no doubt of my genius!"

Mr Penguin felt the only thing here was to nod, so he did.

Mr Chuckle puffed his chest out and started to talk like he was giving a lecture to a rapt audience of people.

"You see, it all started when I was

a child. My father and grandfather became very rich by owning ships – cruise ships like the *Saucy Sandra*, but other ships too, ones that took goods and cargo back and forth across the oceans, and also special ships that set out to explore. These explorations were very successful and the crews of scientists and Adventurers made all manner of incredible discoveries. It was on one of these missions when they found that hideous creature outside and this cave with the treasure within. Here…"

He rummaged around in his pocket for an old sheet of paper, partially unfolded it and handed it to Marina.

"Read this out."

So Marina started to read:

The SS. Snooping Sailor
Explorer Mission No. 345
CAPTAIN'S LOG.

Last night, sailing by the light of a full moon, our team of science officers, the Bunsen sisters, treated us to some most beautiful songs. No sooner had they done so, a ferocious storm began to rage and from fathoms below came a great beast with enormous tentacles and a temper most foul. Our ship was half destroyed by this kraken but we escaped and found ourselves washed up on a small uncharted island.

We sheltered deep within a cave and it was in this hiding place that we made our most incredible discovery.

In the kraken attack, our cabin boy, Albert Skipper, injured his arm most dreadfully and Dr Fionnula Bunsen insisted on using the underground waterfall we discovered to wet a scrap of material and clasp it to the injury. We were amazed to see the badly broken arm miraculously repair itself before our eyes!

We investigated the chamber and discovered a carved inscription upon the wall. Professor Una Bunsen – being an expert in ancient languages – translated it. It read:

Guarded by beast, raised by the moonlight song of seven daughters,

You've discovered the lair of the magical waters.

Scoop from the Fountain – tick-tock – watch time turn,

In the blink of an eye your youth will return*.

Marina stopped reading as she'd got to the bottom of the folded page. Everyone looked at Mr Chuckle, who was grinning like a dog who'd robbed a butcher's. He pointed to the carved letters on the wall of the chamber.

"The crew managed to escape from this island eventually," he explained. "They returned to Cityville and promised never to tell of their discovery – worrying it would endanger people who would try to take on that dangerous monster outside, and also try to take advantage of this miracle water. FOOLS! Didn't they see what treasure it is?

"That captain's log was hidden deep within the library in my grandfather's house. But I grew up hearing whispers of this place and vowed to search it out. I've spent years searching first for that piece of paper in your hand, then for Albert Skipper, the cabin boy – now an old man. He is the only member of the crew still alive, so I tracked him down and he – eventually – confirmed that the report was true. But he wouldn't help me find this place, which is why I had to kidnap him and get my associates to make him talk…"

"You sly, sneaky…" spluttered Marina, trying to find a good word for the awful millionaire. Eventually she settled on "Bumface!" which she shouted with her fists clenched beside her and her cheeks pink with anger.

Beside her, Mr Penguin was doing something he very rarely did – thinking clever thoughts.

"And that's why you invited the Seven Sisters Choir on board the ship!" he said, pleased he had worked something out. "You needed them to sing to get that kraken to swim up to the surface!"

He thought back – every time the sisters had sung, the boat had been rocked about on sudden ferocious waves. Had the sea beast heard the singing each time, and started to wake up? It seemed so.

Colin wanted to add something so he wrote:

YEAH

on his pad and held it up.

Suddenly, there was an explosion from one side of the chamber. Not an actual explosion with dynamite, but something equally as scary – it was

Henry Cutlass, his face twisted.

"ENOUGH WITH THE TALKING!" he shouted. "AND READING!"

He glanced at Colin, who had his marker pen in the air ready to write something.

"AND NOTE-WRITING!" he yelled. "The Fountain of Youth? What rubbish! I think this is all a trick!"

Mr Chuckle snorted like a proud hog.

"You think I'm telling porkies?" he smirked. "Well, why don't we put this fountain to the test?"

And as quick as a flash, the millionaire grabbed hold of Mr Penguin by his rubber ring and hoiked him roughly to the edge of the pool.

CHAPTER TWENTY-FIVE

UNCRINKLED

Great galloping oysters! thought Mr Penguin, his heart clanging like mad in his chest. "He's going to chuck me in the water!"

But the millionaire didn't.

Like a magician, he stopped and wafted a hand in front of Mr Penguin's crinkled, damaged beak. Everyone looked at it, including Mr Penguin (who had to cross his eyes to get a good view). It really was badly out of shape and terribly sore, and he really didn't need everyone eyeballing it.

"Actually," snuffled Mr Penguin, trying to cover it with a flipper, "I'm feeling very self-conscious about it, so if you could all just—"

"Shut up!" snapped Mr Chuckle.

Mr Penguin shut up.

Then, satisfied he had his audience's attention, Mr Chuckle picked up a large, shimmering shell. He dipped it into the pool like a ladle and carefully poured the water over Mr Penguin's beak.

The water was ice cold, but other than that, it didn't seem any different from the water that came from taps back in Cityville.

Everyone held their breath.

Nothing happened.

Henry Cutlass snorted and began to crack his knuckles menacingly.

"See!" he growled. "A trick! Magical waters indeed…"

But then Colin's pad was up in the air.

LOOK!

On the next page he drew an arrow pointing at Mr Penguin.

His beak had started to tingle, then sting a bit like when you rip a plaster off your knee. Everyone gasped as it started to glow as if it was being lit up magically from the inside.

Then, with a
couple of loud creaks
and cracks, his beak
straightened out
and fixed itself
entirely. When it
was finished, it
sparkled briefly and a dainty TING
sound echoed around the chamber,
like someone in a band had struck a
triangle.

Mr Penguin
patted his beak.
It was as good
as new!

"Now!" grinned Mr
Chuckle, his face
gleaming in the
weird glow of
the watery chamber.
"Do you see what
I mean about this
being treasure,
Henry?"

The old man
cast Mr Penguin aside and
started squirrelling about in his
large bag, pulling out handfuls of
empty jars and bottles.

"We are going to fill these up and
sell them! Just think of the money
we'll make! Mountains of the stuff!
Heaps and heaps of it! Who doesn't
want to be young and beautiful?"

Henry Cutlass's face went from

furious red to tickled pink as he caught up with his boss's brilliant plan.

"And we'll be the only ones to know where this place is – everyone else on the ship will be in that monster's belly by now!" he hooted.

Mr Penguin gulped – Edith, Gordon, all the actors and the singing sisters, gobbled up and gone.

"And we'll feed these three meddlers to the kraken!" giggled Mr Chuckle. "Now quickly – we haven't much time. I want to sail back to Cityville and get this stuff into the shops!"

Before they knew it, the three Adventurers found themselves filling up jars with the magical water, screwing the lids on tightly and packing them into the bag. Mr Penguin couldn't believe what was happening – all of this fuss for some water? Was it really worth having an entire ship full of people gobbled up by a sea monster? Wasn't Mr Chuckle rich enough already?

Mr Penguin, feeling actually quite bold, asked the questions aloud.

"Yes, I'm rich!" said Mr Chuckle with a grin. "But you can always be richer! I want to be stinking rich! I want to dive into great piles of gold! And I'll do just that when word gets out about Chuckle's Miraculous Babyface Face Wash! But I need to be fit enough to enjoy all that lovely money. Which is why it's time for Part Two of my plan…"

"Get those back on the

speedboat," he ordered Henry, pointing at the bag.

As the captain headed off with the heavy bag, Mr Chuckle bent to pick up the large shell and filled it to the brim with crystal-clear water.

"Stop!" cried Marina, looking up from the paper she'd been reading. "You shouldn't do that!"

Mr Chuckle ignored her. "Now, it's time to reward my cleverness!" he cried. "I'll be transformed from a ninety-seven-year-old into someone young and handsome again!"

He took a giant swig from the shell cup. Gulp! Gulp! Gulp!

Marina gasped.

"He REALLY shouldn't have done that..." she whispered.

"Why?" asked Mr Penguin and

Colin (on his pad) at exactly the same time.

Mr Penguin noticed that the entire chamber had started to tremble.

But before Marina could answer, two awful things happened.

CHAPTER TWENTY-SIX

ALWAYS READ THE SMALL PRINT

The cave was filled with a tremendous roaring noise.

"Lions?" yelped Mr Penguin, not thinking how a pride of lions would firstly, find the hidden island and then secondly, negotiate the slippery tunnel down to the fountain room. Lions aren't known for their adventuring skills – not like penguins.

Colin tutted, rolled his eyes and the pad was out in an instant.

As it turned out, it wasn't lions (of course it wasn't!) it was...

QUITE A CONSIDERABLE AMOUNT OF WATER

said Colin's pad.

A large plug (that had looked like part of the cave floor) had popped up and from underneath was bubbling up large quantities of salty seawater.

The Fountain of Youth instantly stopped pouring, the carved kraken's mouth clamped shut and the pool of magical water beneath it gurgled away down a drain.

Heavy footprints sounded and Henry Cutlass reappeared from the tunnel, pale-faced, as the entire island seemed to tilt this way and that.

"W-w-what's happening?" he demanded.

The water from the plughole was now sloshing about at ankle height, and the whole island was still rocking back and forth.

Mr Penguin, being a polite sort and wanting to answer the question, just pointed to Marina. She'd know.

"It's all on here!" she said, raising her voice over the rushing water. "It's in the small print! Look!"

She started to read aloud from her piece of paper:

*Use only what you need, then depart from this lair,
Thieves and the greedy, be careful!
BEWARE!*

The water must stay here – just where it ought'a
Or the island will sink back under the water!

"What does that mean?" cried Mr Penguin, the water up to his bum now.

"It means because Henry took the water out of the chamber…"

"The island is now SINKING!" squeaked Mr Penguin, catching on.

"And…" said Marina.

"It gets worse?" croaked Mr Penguin, nearly fainting. Colin caught him and wafted his friend's panicking face with his pad.

"I'm afraid so…" continued Marina. "Didn't you read ALL of this, Mr Chuckle?"

Everyone turned to face the

millionaire and their jaws hit the floor.

The air around Mr Chuckle was snapping and fizzing, just as it had when Mr Penguin's beak was being healed, but with much more excitement and electricity this time. The chamber was flickering with ancient magic. As the captain and the Adventurers watched, the tiny elderly man started to glow, rising into the air.

I DO NOT THINK HE READ ALL OF IT

said Colin helpfully.

"Oh no…" muttered Marina.

The old man floated above the chamber, a bubble of green, glowing magic forming around him. His body started to transform, like a puppet with invisible strings being bobbled about by a mad puppeteer. His wrinkly face

smoothed like it was being flattened by
an invisible iron, and his back
straightened, accompanied by several
large and uncomfortable-sounding
clicks. His legs and arms grew long and

smooth again – so much so that his snazzy suit trousers were suddenly like a pair of shorts. His hair was revealed to be a little wig, popping off the top of his head and vanishing into thin air. His bald pate suddenly sprouted great tufts of thick glistening hair. It was incredible! It was miraculous! It was...

"SCARY!" shouted Mr Penguin over the roar of water.

But it wasn't over yet...

CHAPTER TWENTY-SEVEN

EVEN
SMALLER
PRINT

Inside the bubble, Mr Chuckle started to laugh giddily, marvelling at his new, youthful body. He turned somersaults in the glowing orb.

"I'm young again!" he hooted.
"Young and gorgeous! I'll be richer
and more famous than ever before!
All my life's work for this wondrous,
wondrous moment!"

The cave rocked violently again
and the water bubbling up from the
plughole seemed to double in speed.
Mr Penguin and Marina were
knocked off their feet, saved by Colin
who swirled a loop of webbing and
tugged them to a rock nearby. They
scrambled up it, glad to be
momentarily out of the rising tide.

From the mouth of the tunnel,
Henry Cutlass took one look at the
madness in front of him, threw the
bag of jam jars to the floor and
skedaddled back up the slippery
corridor.

Mr Chuckle stopped his celebrations and seemed for the first time to notice that the room was rapidly filling with water.

"We need to leave now!" he cried, poking at the bubble surrounding him.

Nothing happened.

"What?" he cried, poking it harder this time. "Why won't it break? Wait – w-w-what's happening now?"

Mr Chuckle started to glow so brightly Mr Penguin couldn't look – not without his sunglasses which, OF COURSE, he'd left in his cabin.

Mr Penguin turned to Marina. "Why won't it break?" he hissed.

"Because he didn't read the even smaller print! He didn't bother to unfold the paper and read EVERYTHING," she said.

She pointed at a sentence written in LARGE CAPITAL LETTERS. Mr Penguin started to read:

WARNING:
THE FOUNTAIN OF YOUTH
IS FOR EXTERNAL USE ONLY.

Water sploshed over the text, making the ink unreadable.

"Or else what?" said Mr Penguin.

THAT…

said Colin's pad. He scrambled back through the pages to find his arrow from earlier, and waggled it at the glowing bubble containing Mr Chuckle.

The glowing stopped. It was like a lamp had been switched off.

Mr Penguin gasped.

Mr Chuckle was no longer inside the orb. Well, he was, but he wasn't the same. He'd been transformed into…

CHAPTER TWENTY-EIGHT

UNEXPECTED RESULTS

"A BABY!"

The three Adventurers gasped. Inside the bubble, illuminated by the dim blue-green light of the coral chandelier above them, was now a baby.

It looked at the three pals, grinned and waved a chubby hand in their direction.

Despite the great danger they were in, Mr Penguin, Marina and Colin all slowly waved back.

The baby chuckled and floated about until its bare bottom was facing the pals, waggled it in their direction and hooted with laughter.

"What HAPPENED to Mr Chuckle?" asked Mr Penguin, agog.

"He was greedy!" said Marina, pulling Mr Penguin further up the rock and away from the rushing water. Colin clambered up beside her. "He didn't bother to read ALL the instructions."

With a lurch of his stomach, Mr Penguin noticed that the water was

rising towards their one escape from the underground room – the entrance to the tunnel.

I THINK IT WOULD BE A GOOD IDEA IF WE LEFT HERE NOW

said Colin on his pad.

"We'll have to swim for it!" said Marina, rolling up her sleeves.

Mr Penguin groaned.

Then suddenly there was a loud POP! as the bubble holding the baby (formerly known as Mr Herbert Chuckle) burst, and the infant millionaire dropped like a stone into the water below.

He bobbed to the surface again (thank goodness!) and started to cry.

"We can't leave him!" cried Mr Penguin over the noise of the water and the wailing baby.

The adult Mr Chuckle had been really awful, but he couldn't be left to swim out by himself. Would he even know how? Mr Penguin didn't know very much about babies.

Above their heads, the coral chandelier started to creak ominously and the blue-green lights began going out with a fizz. Within a few minutes, the baby Mr Chuckle and the three Adventurers would be hurled against the pointy stalactites on the ceiling of the chamber.

"We'll have to swim to him," said Marina, but the words were hardly out of her mouth when the water started to swirl about to form a huge, churning whirlpool. Baby Chuckle was hurled towards another rock that was just about poking above the water. He gripped it with his pudgy little fingers.

Mr Penguin started to do his panicky little dance on top of the slippy rock island. It was quite difficult to do, but he was somehow managing.

They couldn't swim through a whirlpool! It was too treacherous. They would be sucked into it and thrown to the bottom of the sea under gallons and gallons of water.

All hope seemed lost.

This was worse than the other day when he and Colin had had to rescue Gordon when he was knocked overboard. As dangerous as that had been, at least the waves had only been going up and down, not round and round like this whirlpool.

Suddenly, he stopped and gasped.

That was it!

Mr Penguin had An Idea…

CHAPTER TWENTY-NINE

SWINGING AND DANGLING

Mr Penguin quickly explained his idea to his chums.

After Colin had written:

GOBSMACKED GASP

on his pad and held it up, and Marina had hooted with relief, they set to work.

Colin clambered into Marina's cupped hands. With an "OOF!" she hurled him up towards the roof of the chamber, where he landed daintily on the coral chandelier. He let out a burst of webbing from his bottom and tied it firmly around the thick central frond of coral. He tugged on it briefly to make sure it was secure (it was!) before leaping back towards his chums.

On top of their rock, Mr Penguin and Marina were ready. Colin landed on Mr Penguin and quickly knotted the strand of webbing he'd brought with him around his pal's belly. When it was knotted tight, Mr Penguin and Colin leapt into the air, and Marina helped them on their way with a terrific shove.

They swung out over the

whirlpool, swirling and roaring beneath them, and towards Baby Chuckle. The infant millionaire was still just about gripping on to the pointy bit of a stalagmite island.

Mr Penguin stretched out his flippers towards the baby. STREEEEEETCCCCCH! But try as he might he couldn't quite reach his target.

Baby Chuckle looked at his almost rescuer with big, blinking, puppy-dog eyes, and his little lip started to wobble.

"DON'T WORRY MR – ER, MASTER CHUCKLE!" cried Mr Penguin, now completely upside down. "I'LL BE BACK IN A JIFFY, WON'T I, COLIN?"

Frantic jottings as Colin wrote:
YES
on his pad, and the two

Adventurers swung violently back towards Marina.

She was ready for them. Eyebrows furrowed, sleeves rolled back and with a determined grimace on her fizzog, she gave her two pals another almighty shove.

Mr Penguin and Colin hurtled across the room and, just as Baby Chuckle's grip on his rocky moorings weakened and his fingers pinged off one by one, Mr Penguin grabbed him and tucked his wiggling bottom securely under one of his flippers!

"HOORAY!" hooted Mr Penguin. "Now let's grab Marina and scram!"

But that was easier said than done.

It was as if the chamber somehow knew Mr Penguin and his pals were about to escape and take the greedy Mr Chuckle (now an innocent baby) with them. It seemed to tremble with anger.

The water filling the room rose at a tremendous rate and the whirlpool doubled in speed. The stalactites started to plummet into the waves, knocking Marina off her perch and into the water.

"HELP!" she cried.

Mr Penguin's eyes shot to his friend. She was in danger! He glanced at Colin where the pad was already out.

WIGGLE YOUR BUM.

Mr Penguin didn't argue. He wiggled his bottom with all his might. Slowly they managed to pick up enough momentum to start swinging across the chamber again. Under his flipper, the baby Mr Chuckle stopped crying and started to giggle.

"Oh!" cried Mr Penguin, delighted. "He likes this!"

FOR GOODNESS' SAKE CONCENTRATE, MR PENGUIN said the pad.

Mr Penguin furrowed his brow and wiggled harder. With a final swing they sailed right above Marina and with another huge streeeeeeetch, Mr Penguin grabbed her hand.

"Excellent teamwork!" Marina yelled, between mouthfuls of seawater. "Now – to the tunnel!"

They swung with all their might before, with one final push, they landed with a clatter in the entrance of the rocky tunnel.

They leapt to their feet, all relieved to feel dry(ish) ground beneath them. Marina grabbed the webbing still connecting Colin to the coral and the spider snapped it, freeing himself.

"What now?" asked Mr Penguin, hoping that maybe Marina might have a little nibble of some food in her pocket or something that could just Sustain and Revive him before what was, he thought with a sigh, probably also going to be highly dangerous.

"Up and out, of course!" said Marina, leading the way. "Quick! Before the water follows—"

But she didn't manage to say the last word of that sentence (which was "us", by the way) because the water DID follow them. It threw itself at the entrance of the tunnel, filling it up, and the three Adventurers and the baby were hurled at breakneck speed back

up the rocky corridor, ricocheting
around each twist and turn before

POP!

WHOOSH!

they shot out of the cave entrance and
into the air above the ocean like a cork
from an enormous, shaken-up bottle of
champagne.

CHAPTER THIRTY

A GHOST SHIP

The gang of Adventurers and the baby (who roared with laughter as they sailed through the air) landed with a gigantic splash before all bobbing up to the surface like a raft of rubber ducks. Behind them there was a tremendous glugging sound as the final rocky tip of the mysterious island disappeared beneath the waves, and all that remained was a few bubbles.

Mr Penguin opened his eyes and found that everything was black.

"Oh my cod and chips!" he cried out, his tummy gurgling with hunger and panic. "Where are we now? Inside the belly of the kraken?" He didn't remember being eaten, but then he'd seen so many strange things during the last few hours that nothing would have surprised him.

"Um... Mr Penguin," Marina said. "I think you might see better if you take your flippers from in front of your eyes..."

Oh, thought Mr Penguin, and he found that yes, she was right. He wasn't in a sea monster's belly at all! He slowly looked around.

It was dawn now and the sky was the colour of a dirty dishcloth. A thick, chilly mist was hanging low over the water. Beside him, Marina was holding on to Baby Chuckle, who was happily splashing Colin (who wasn't enjoying it at all). Everything was silent and actually quite creepy.

Thankfully, the kraken was nowhere to be seen, but the gigantic brute was probably underneath their paddling feet right at that very moment. Was it going to gobble them up for breakfast?

Mr Penguin quivered in his rubber ring.

All around them were broken bits
of the *Saucy Sandra* – splintered
wooden floorboards and tattered pieces
of rope. And, floating in front of them,
the smashed remains of Mr Chuckle's
model *Saucy Sandra*.

Colin tapped Mr Penguin and
pointed at a dark shape, coming
through the fog like a ghost.

It was the *Saucy Sandra*!

Miraculously, it was still just about afloat. It was in a dreadful state – all battered and buckled and not at all like the smart ship that had set sail just a few days ago.

"What do we do now?" Mr Penguin whispered.

The three Adventurers looked at each other. Apart from the mess and the very sad-looking ship, the only thing around them was miles of steel-grey, freezing ocean.

Scribblings.

WE NEED TO GO ON BOARD THE SHIP TO SEE WHAT'S

Next page:

WHAT.

Mr Penguin gulped. He supposed it would be quite nice to get out of the sea to towel off his brogues (if there was a dry towel to be found on board), so he let Colin propel him towards the ship.

The Adventurers and Baby Chuckle (tucked once again under Mr Penguin's flipper) paddled to the boat and clambered up the side with the help of a line of strong web.

Mr Penguin couldn't help himself thinking Very Worrying Thoughts.

What would they find on board? From the eerie silence he supposed nothing at all. And if the ship WERE empty, where were his friends? What had happened to Edith and Gordon and the Seven Sisters Choir and the Hollywoodland film stars?

The gang edged along the deck. There were enormous holes in it and what was left of the handrails was bent completely out of shape.

Their footsteps echoed in the gloom. Mr Penguin was just about to do what he always did in a real crisis – throw himself beak-down on the floor – when there came a noise.

It was a voice – a solitary voice in the grey, damp quiet.

"I know it's a bit soggy now…" it said matter-of-factly. The three Adventurers stopped and cocked their ears to listen.

The voice continued:

"But there's a large spanner in my bumbag that will fix it."

BUMBAG?!

Surely that could be only one person!

CHAPTER THIRTY-ONE

A BUSY SORT
OF EVENING

"EDITH!" cried Mr Penguin and Colin (on his pad) at the same time.

And the gang all raced as fast as they could to where the voice was coming from – it seemed to be in what was left of Mr Chuckle's office.

They burst through the door (which was easy because it was hanging off its hinges). Mr Penguin couldn't believe what he was seeing! His heart did a wild, jigging Charleston dance.

There was Edith – jolly as always – standing on Mr Chuckle's desk, bunging up a leaky pipe above her with a pair of nylons in one hand whilst rummaging through her bumbag with the other. Gordon was sitting on her head looking in two different directions at once as usual.

But there was someone else in the room. He was standing in front of a large hole in the wall, looking at a large sheet of paper that appeared to be a plan of the ship and scratching his head. He looked up and a great grin spread across his face.

"GRAMPA!" hooted Marina. She threw her arms around him, whipping the hat from her head and plonking it on his.

For the next minute or so, there was a huge amount of hugging and jumping about with excitement. Mr Penguin hugged Edith and Gordon. Marina hugged her grampa and then Albert Skipper hugged Mr Penguin.

Colin formally shook everyone's hands with his hand-feet.

"We thought you'd been gobbled up by that sea monster!" said Mr Penguin, hardly believing that his friends were there, definitely ungobbled.

Then Mr Penguin thought of something awful – what about the rest of the passengers? The film stars and the singing sisters? The mayor and the police chief?

"Everyone's safe!" said Edith. "Don't worry about that! Albert and I have sent them all to bed – we've had a busy sort of an evening. Everyone was tired and those film stars start arguing with each other when they need a sleep…"

"But what about the pirate crew?"

asked Marina.

Mr Penguin gasped. He'd almost forgotten about them. Where were they? Would they suddenly appear, snarling and cracking their knuckles, and throw the Adventurers to the sharks?

Edith grinned, her whole face crinkling up like a walnut.

"Oh! We won't have any more trouble from them, will we, Albert? Look!"

And Edith pointed at a hole in the floor. Everyone gathered around it and peered down into the room below. Sitting in a circle, bound tightly with rope, were all the pirates. Gone were their menacing snarls. Instead, they all looked very sheepish and sorry for themselves. Henry Cutlass was looking as meek as a mouse.

Edith hooted with laughter. "Would you believe he came sailing back to the ship in a speedboat? And actually ASKED to be rescued and tied up with the rest of them. Said he'd had a very frightening experience in a cave and that going to jail would be more peaceful than being a pirate!"

"When we get this ship fixed and back to Cityville, we'll hand them over to the police," said Albert.

"You did all of this by yourselves?" Mr Penguin said, flabbergasted. In fact, he couldn't remember the last time his flabber had ever been so gasted.

"Well..." said Edith, winking at Albert. "We had a tiny bit of help from a new friend."

"Who?" asked Marina.

"Me!" said a voice from behind them.

The gang spun on their heels to see someone coming through the door.

CHAPTER THIRTY-TWO

MOJITO JONES

"HONEY CRYSTELLE?!" cried Mr Penguin, backing away in terror as the glamorous woman came into the room.

Actually, once she came into the light, she wasn't looking quite so glamorous. Her hair was in what looked like a napkin and, like Edith, there was engine oil smeared across her face. A spanner was tucked under her arm and in her hands was a tea tray with a hot teapot and a pile of slightly chipped cups. She was still wearing her sparkly party frock though, so all in all she looked quite a sight.

Mr Penguin had to admit that she did look much less stern than before – almost friendly – but he didn't understand. He'd seen her get into the lifeboat when the kraken attacked last night, and before that she had been sneaking about and acting very suspiciously. Yet here was Edith calling her a new friend!

"But… But… But…" he stammered. "You're…"

Honey grinned and started to pour the tea.

"Go on," said Edith. "Tell him!"

"Well," said Honey matter-of-factly, "I'm actually a secret agent!"

Mr Penguin and Marina gasped. Colin GASP-ed on his pad then quickly turned the page and wrote:

WELL I

Next page:

NEVER.

"And," the secret agent continued, spooning three large sugars into Mr Penguin's cup as he stood, beak flapping, "I'm not really called Honey Crystelle. The name's Jones, Mojito Jones."

Mr Penguin found his flipper being shaken by her firm hand. All he could say was "Huh?"

Colin rolled his eyes.

"I think I'd better do some explaining…" said Honey-Who-Was-Now-Actually-Called-Mojito-Jones. Then she turned to look at the baby, who had curled up and fallen asleep. In the excitement, he'd almost been forgotten.

"Actually," Mojito Jones said, "I think we ALL have some explaining to do!"

They moved to the comfort of the restaurant so the pirates couldn't overhear them, and then everyone chit-chattered nonstop.

Marina, Mr Penguin and Colin told the others about what had happened on the island – the hidden chamber, Mr Chuckle's dreadful plan, the Fountain of Youth and Mr Penguin's wonky beak being fixed by the magical waters.

Albert nodded. It was all as he remembered it from when he was a boy.

Finally, the three Adventurers told Edith, Albert and Mojito about how Herbert Chuckle came to be the baby, now snoring peacefully.

Mojito Jones looked very serious.

"He was *very* greedy," she said,

shaking her head. "I always thought it might be his downfall. I didn't know that THIS was what he was planning – I'm just very glad that no one else got hurt."

Then she went on to tell the gang about her involvement in the case.

She really was a secret agent who had been assigned to investigate Mr Chuckle. For several years he had definitely been Up To Something – making suspicious enquiries, asking odd questions at the city library about uncharted islands.

Mojito Jones, pretending to be Miss Honey Crystelle, got to know Mr Chuckle and was able to spy on his plans. He'd had one of his father's old boats painted to look new (he wasn't going to waste a nice new boat on a dangerous mission) and hired the pirate crew.

She'd only found out that Albert Skipper had been kidnapped once the ship had set sail, and that's why she, like Marina, had also been snooping around the ship – firstly to find out where he was, and secondly to find the keys. When Mr Penguin had seen her coming out of Mr Chuckle's office before the party, she'd snuck in to have one last look for the keys.

Henry Cutlass had admitted that the reason she couldn't find them was that he had taken to keeping them tucked in his underpants for safe keeping.

"Then how did you get Mr Skipper free?" asked Mr Penguin,

thinking that picking all the locks on the octopus door would have taken ages.

"Oh, that was easy in the end," said Edith, tapping her bumbag. "I just took the door off its hinges and out popped Albert, ready to help us deal with the madness of last night!"

Besides the kraken walloping

the *Saucy Sandra* like a lunatic, the remaining pirate crew had been spitting angry when they'd discovered that the second speedboat had been glued solid to the deck! Mr Chuckle hadn't wanted to share his treasure and had hoped that they too would be gobbled up by the kraken.

"So," said Edith, pouring everyone another cup of tea, "we had a sea monster and a furious crew of pirates to deal with AS WELL as the choir and the film stars and the mayor and the police chief all panicking!"

"Which was why I leapt from the speedboat and swam back to the *Saucy Sandra* to help out," said Mojito Jones. "I couldn't have a ship full of people swallowed up because Herbert had some greedy scheme up his sleeve. So

Edith and Gordon freed Albert and he steered the ship out of the way of those tentacles, then they busied themselves getting the kraken under control. I used my secret agent kung fu skills to stop those rogues downstairs being dastardly and pirate-y, and got them tied up tight so they wouldn't cause us any more problems."

"Oh, you should've seen her!" chuckled Edith. "Her kung fu skills are ALMOST as good as yours, Colin!"

At this Colin beamed and just drew a love heart on his pad and held it up.

"We were so worried that you'd all been eaten by that monster!" said Marina, patting her grampa's arm almost as if to check that he was still there.

Albert laughed. "Oh, there was never any danger of that!" he hooted. "As I kept trying to tell Mr Chuckle, a kraken would never eat PEOPLE. It's vegetarian. Seaweed mostly, I think. We found that out all those years ago when I was a boy and it was only interested in getting to our cargo – boxes and boxes of fruit!"

Urgh! thought Mr Penguin. Fancy eating fruit by choice.

It certainly had been a busy evening, but there were two things still confusing Mr Penguin.

He understood why the Ladies' Choir had been invited on board – Mr Chuckle had needed them to raise the kraken from its sleep – but why invite all the Hollywoodland stars and the mayor and the police chief?

"Aha!" said Mojito. "I didn't know exactly what Herbert's plan was, but I knew that once he'd found his treasure, that was only the beginning. He was so jealous of the film stars – they were much younger than him—"

"And they are all VERY handsome!" added Edith, wafting her face with a saucer.

"Well, yes," continued Mojito. "That too, I suppose. I think, now I know that he'd been planning on making himself young again, that he wanted them out of the way so that once he was back in Cityville he could start making himself a film star. He wasn't just greedy for more money and being young again, he was greedy for power. I guess he invited the mayor so he could get her out of the way and then be the mayor instead. And getting the police chief out of the way meant that no one would be able to stop his schemes. Who knows... maybe he was one day even planning on being the president!"

Mr Penguin nodded his head. The only problem left was what to do with the infant Chuckle. He'd been a dastardly scheming old man, but now he was just a baby. Mr Penguin couldn't look after him. His igloo was far too small, and besides, he'd never be able to do his adventuring while pushing a pram. And he didn't really fancy changing nappies.

Edith couldn't look after him because as well as being in Mr

Penguin's gang, when she was back in Cityville she was terribly busy with the pigeons in the park.

Mojito Jones couldn't look after Mr Chuckle because she was a very important secret agent with missions to complete – and besides, she didn't really like babies.

"So where is he going to live?" asked Albert.

What this baby needed, Mr Penguin thought, was somewhere jolly where he'd be looked after by kind people who would make him kind in turn.

His thoughts were interrupted by someone knocking at the door and saying, "Coo-ee! Can we come in?"

It was the Ladies Choir, awake and ready with their sleeves pushed up to help fix the ship. They were soon clucking like hens over Baby Chuckle who woke up, giggling, to find his chin being tickled by the seven ladies.

As he watched them, Mr Penguin suddenly had a very clever idea indeed.

CHAPTER THIRTY-THREE

GORDON'S
SECRET

The next twenty-four hours were a blur of activity.

The first thing that happened was that Mojito Jones took full control and set about concocting a story – to explain the disappearance of Mr Chuckle and the arrival on board of a baby – firstly for the passengers, and then for the newspaper people who would no doubt be at Cityville Docks on their return. (She had, in her secret agent kit, a telegram machine, so she used that to tell the police to be ready for the pirates.)

She thought Mr Penguin's idea for the baby Mr Chuckle was excellent, so she got that all fixed up too. The Adventurers promised never to tell a soul what really happened on the island – not even the sisters or the film stars. Mojito Jones – being very firm and Not-To-Be-Argued-With – got everyone to agree to keep the kraken attack a secret.

If people found out about a sea monster, she said, they would be terrified and then want to find it and capture it and probably hurt it, and all it really wanted to do was have a nice sleep under the sea.

Instead they would say that the boat had been battered about in a ferocious storm, which was partly true. Or true enough.

The next job was to finish fixing the *Saucy Sandra* so it could get home safely.

Everyone worked very hard indeed, hammering and spannering and generally patching the boat up. Despite being exhausted, Mr Penguin turned his attention to what he felt was the MOST important job of all – finding some food. His stomach was roaring like a dragon, and he was quite dizzy from it.

He'd been right the other day when he'd thought there was less food about than there had been – Mr Chuckle had only provided enough food until the full moon party and the kraken's arrival. After that there would be no need for a full larder since, had his scheme gone to plan, the ship would have been sitting at the bottom of the ocean.

Mr Penguin gathered up what he could find, as well as discovering that the lifeboat Henry Cutlass had used to paddle frantically back to the *Saucy Sandra* had a pile of food tucked under the seat.

TO FEED MR CHUCKLE ON HIS WAY BACK TO CITYVILLE NO DOUBT

Colin deduced on his pad.

Finally, Mr Penguin had been delighted to find that his heavy trunk was still in his cabin, undamaged by the kraken's attack. In it he'd packed The Essentials. Instead of spare pants and socks, there were MOUNDS of food he'd packed just in case they needed them. And oh boy did they!

Once he'd practically swallowed a tin of sardines whole – metal container and all – he dragged all the food into the dining room and everyone tucked in whilst they waited for the engines to fire up.

Mr Penguin found himself sitting next to Edith, who was happily munching away and tidying her tools away in her bumbag. The last thing she did was pull out a little compact, open it up and look at herself in the mirror. With a lick of the thumb she wiped away some engine oil from her nose.

Mr Penguin looked at his friend's face. It was just as wrinkled as Mr Chuckle's had been.

"Edith?" asked Mr Penguin, rubbing his beak thoughtfully. "If you could have made yourself young again with that magical water, would you have done it?"

Edith looked aghast.

"And get rid of all my lovely wrinkles?" she cried, tapping her face happily. "No thank you! The very idea!"

She admired her face in the glass and smiled.

"Each one of these lines is a little souvenir of all the adventures I've had and all the laughs I've hooted," she said. "And I'm very keen on making more of them! There's something so nice about getting older. It's like an adventure itself! Hopefully…" and she whispered the next bit, "Mr Chuckle will understand that the second time around."

She popped her mirror away and

got stuck into what was turning into quite a little party in the ship's dining room – much more fun than the one that the kraken had interrupted the other evening.

Whilst Mr Penguin was thinking about the sea monster, a niggling little question popped into his head. How exactly HAD Edith and Gordon calmed the kraken down? It had been in a ferocious temper.

He asked Edith, as she helped herself to some more cookies from Mr Penguin's emergency stash. She grinned broadly and, behaving like a furtive ferret, pulled Mr Penguin and Colin out on deck.

"Well…" she whispered. "It turns out that Gordon here has a bit of a secret himself."

They looked at Gordon. The pigeon looked back at them with one eye whilst the other one careered around wildly.

Mr Penguin was flummoxed. What secret could his odd little friend be keeping?

"He'd been acting strangely since we came on board," hissed Edith. "You remember how he was always listening to the swimming pool, and almost got his head stuck in a glass of water? Well… Gordon could hear that sea monster grumbling under the sea and was trying to communicate with it."

Mr Penguin and Colin just blinked.

"Yes," continued Edith. "It turns out that Gordon can speak kraken."

More stunned blinking.

Edith looked surreptitiously over her shoulder to check that everyone else was still busy in the dining room. The chatting and laughter coming from them was very loud indeed. Satisfied they were all distracted, Edith said:

"Go on, Gord, show Mr Penguin and Colin your trick…"

Gordon stood up on Edith's head, ruffled his feathers and honked like a foghorn.

Nothing happened for a moment, then the ship began rocking gently as large bubbles appeared in the sea nearby. Then two large, sleepy eyes appeared above the surface. It was the kraken – not angry this time, just very sleepy – and, Mr Penguin thought, looking rather sheepish.

It waved a tentacle at the

Adventurers, who, stunned, waved back.

Edith chucked it a cookie, which it caught and happily gobbled before waving wearily again.

With glugging sounds and more bubbles, the sea monster disappeared below the surface.

"One hoot from Gordon calmed that beastie right down," said Edith, giving Gordon a handful of cookie crumbs. "I don't know what Gordon said to it, but it swam off as quiet as a lamb!"

Mr Penguin continued to blink.
Even Colin was lost for words, his
pen hovering uselessly in midair.

Eventually the pals gave up
looking for the words they
needed, and decided to
go back inside and
enjoy the party.

Just after midnight, the *Saucy Sandra*'s engines were ready and the Adventurers took their place in the wheelhouse beside Marina and her grampa, who would be steering the boat back to dry land. Mojito Jones had scurried off to disguise herself with sunglasses and a trench coat so she would be ready to slip away unnoticed (as a good secret agent should) from the boat when they returned.

Sitting in the cabin, Mr Penguin thought excitedly of all the things he would do when he got back to his igloo. First of all there would be several fish finger sandwiches to be gobbled, followed by a long nap in his hammock.

He wiggled with pleasure, thinking about the nice few days'

holiday he would have – to recover
from this holiday that turned out not
to be a holiday at all!

On Albert's nod, Mr Penguin
pulled a handle hard and an enormous
PAAAAARP filled the night sky. The
Saucy Sandra started to sail home.

But little did Mr Penguin know
that back in his igloo, on the front-
door mat sat a teetering pile of
envelopes, and in each one was a new
adventure URGENTLY needing to be
dealt with…

THE END

(Until the next next time!)

Aaah… peace at last.

Just the gentle bubbly glugging as the fish swim by and the seaweed sways like a nice lullaby…

Good that the annoying singing has stopped and you can get back to doing what you do best – guarding that little secret island…

You feel a bit embarrassed at the mess you made of that nice boat, but that's what happens when you wake up feeling grumpy…

And it wasn't all bad. There was that strange feathery sort of fish sitting on that person's head…

A strange feathery fish who spoke
to you so sweetly and asked, very
nicely, if you wouldn't mind not
attacking the boat…
    You said it would be your
pleasure.
        And now here you are again…
Fathoms below…
            Drifting off to sleep…
            Where you'll dream of your
            new little friend – a strange
            feathery sort of fish…

The Cityville Times

MORNING EDITION

15th DECEMBER

DRAMA ON THE HIGH SEAS!

There were dramatic scenes yesterday as the *Saucy Sandra* limped back to the Cityville Docks, barely held together after being nearly shipwrecked in a storm. The safe return of the ship has been credited to retired sailor Albert Skipper and Cityville's In-The-Centre Park's bird warden, Edith Hedge, who used their nautical know-how to save the day!

According to the guests, the storm struck the ship just after midnight a few days ago whilst the passengers and crew partied under the full moon.

The famous Mr Penguin was amongst the passengers and spoke to the crowds of reporters as the boat docked.

The Adventurer said, "The storm hit us just as the canapés were served, which was a shame really as they looked tasty. There was thunder and lightning and enormous waves. But there were definitely

no sea monsters AHAHAHAHAHA HAHAHA! No, none of them. Just an awful storm."

Mr Penguin added, "I don't suppose anyone has a fish finger sandwich about their person, do they? I'm absolutely ravenous."

DRAMA ON THE HIGH SEAS!

wasn't all bad news. During the storm, the passengers discovered a baby boy bobbing about in the ocean in a box. Brave young Adventurer Marina Skipper swam and brought the baby to safety. Where the child came from is a mystery.

The happy ending continues with the news that the boy, who has been named after the ship's owner, Herbert Chuckle, was adopted by the Cityville Ladies Choir and live with them at Fluffy Cuddles House. As this report went to print, the baby was being smothered with kisses and cuddles by his seven adoring mothers.

MISSING PASSENGERS!

Unfortunately, the *Saucy Sandra* brought with it some distressing news. It appears that the city's Cinema King Mr Herbert Chuckle (97) and his girlfriend, Miss Honey Crystelle, were thrown overboard and remain lost at sea.

A glamorous passenger, dressed in sunglasses and a trench coat, told reporters she imagined neither of the missing people would ever be found again and would probably live the rest of their lives on a desert island and be very happy, so not to worry too much about finding them.

Thank you to Danielle Pinnock-Wallace for her lovely, kind and helpful advice. Thank you to Janine and Mr Penguin's brilliant crew: Alison Still, Alison Eldred, Rachel Wade and Emma Mayfield. Mr Danton Eyre sends his thanks to Mr Matthew Land.

ALSO BY ALEX T. SMITH

CLAUDE

Meet Claude – no ordinary dog!
When his owners, Mr and Mrs
Shinyshoes, go to work, the fun
begins for Claude and his best
friend Sir Bobblysock.

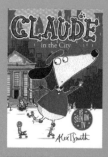

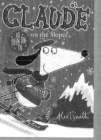

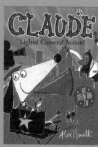